Onyx

by

Debbie Izzo

DORRANCE PUBLISHING CO., INC.
PITTSBURGH, PENNSYLVANIA 15222

ISBN: 978-1-4349-0741-7
Printed in the United States of America

First Printing

For more information or to order additional books, please contact:
Dorrance Publishing Co., Inc.
701 Smithfield Street
Pittsburgh, Pennsylvania 15222
U.S.A.
1-800-788-7654
www.dorrancebookstore.com

Acknowledgements

I would like to thank my niece, Colleen, whose suggestions helped pull my ideas into this book.

I would like to thank Victoria for being my first audience.

And I would like to thank my husband, Rich, and my children, Richard and Laura, for believing in me.

Chapter 1
Adjoining

I never believed in fate or destiny. I just lived each day one at a time, existing. I was told God made each person with a special purpose in mind. My purpose escaped me. I was also taught people come in and out of your life, changing its fabric, weaving their threads into yours, and binding their impression indelibly on you. I never really knew what that statement meant. How could I? I never met anyone who had that kind of impact on me. But my life was about to change. Someone would enter my life, twisting my destiny beyond my control.

My name is Allyson Katherine Baker. I hated my name almost as much as I hated my dead-end life and being unforgettably usual. My brothers teasingly nicknamed me Ally Kat. The moniker just reinforced my feelings of inadequacy. I often felt like an alley cat, some discarded remnant of life aimlessly wandering in search of a home, harbor, or somewhere I belonged.

I suppose I should have been grateful for my family. They taught me so much. I learned to share because there wasn't any space to call my own. I learned to be giving because if you didn't give it would be taken. And most of all, I learned I was invisible.

It all started the summer before I turned seventeen. Being sixteen should have been a great time in my life, a time filled with firsts: first time driving, first date, first kiss, first love. But being invisible smothered all hope I would experience any of that. Economics prevented me from getting a car. My parents had an army of children to support, and I only had a part-time job babysitting the neighbor's children. A car was definitely out of the question.

As for the romance department, I would have to become visible before it could ever happen. I suppose it was unfair of me to hope for anything else. I had been blessed with an ordinary appearance. I stood barely five foot three in height. My stature allowed me to easily be lost in a crowd. My hair was a bland, nondescript light brown. I kept it braided in a long cord running the length of my back like a symbolic rope tying me to my existence. My eyes couldn't even decide on a color. They seemed to rock back and forth between green, blue, and hazel depending on the color of clothing I wore. My clothes were usually jeans and a shirt most likely purchased at a Goodwill store because it was all I could afford. The only feature that made me slightly different was my build, but I would have preferred being usual instead. I was blessed with curves. Other girls were beautifully, anorexical thin, a stick to hang clothes on. I went in and out in a figure eight, a body style out of fashion decades ago.

My parents had seven children —one for every day of the week, my father would joke. I was sandwiched between brothers until my cousin, Samantha, came to live with us ten years ago. Samantha was the only child of my dad's brother. Uncle John and his wife had died in a car accident when I was six, and my father became Samantha's legal guardian.

Samantha was the best thing that ever happened to me. Until Sam came, I had no one to talk to. Sam was six years older than me, but we were sisters of the soul. Right from the start, Sam and I shared a common bond. She was invisible too. We had the same interests, sense of humor, and mannerisms. People who met us really thought we were sisters. The only difference between us was Sam wore her hair short and my hair reached my waist.

It was wonderful growing up with Sam. She always looked out for me just like a big sister. She left a massive void in my life when she left to go to college four years ago. Of course she wrote and called me, but it wasn't the same as being together. I had waited patiently for her to graduate and move back home, but a month ago she shocked the family. She called to say she had met someone, Don Saltate, and they had eloped. After that she sounded different, not the Sam I had shared so much with.

Sam's elopement scandalized the family. The gossip caused by this frivolous act ran uncontrollably like wild fire through my family and our other relatives. My father was extremely upset, and I didn't see how he ever would forgive her for the embarrassment she caused him.

It had taken more than a month, but the furor over Sam's action was finally dying down. We didn't talk about Samantha anymore. I feared she would drift from my life, and I would never see her again.

Samantha must have sensed the cold reception to her marriage and broke off all contact with the family. So I was shocked and grateful when she called.

"Hello, little sis. I really missed you," she began.

"Oh my God, Samantha, I thought you forgot all about me."

"I couldn't forget about you. We are sisters, aren't we? I know I have been busy since I got married, and I have neglected you. I'm sorry. I've thought about you every day. I really miss talking to you. I know your father is still pretty mad at me, so I didn't call the house. I'm hoping staying clear and giving him time will help settle things."

"I tried to call you at school, in your dorm room, but I was only able to leave messages with your roommate. Did you get them?"

"I did, but once I met Don, I forgot about everything else. I'm sorry. I can't wait for you to meet him. He is the most wonderful, handsome, perfect man I have ever met. You'll think I invented him, he is so perfect."

I could tell Don would change my relationship with Sam. She was in love. I could hear it in her voice. She had someone to fill her heart and mind completely. How could I ever compete with him?

I continued the conversation, cherishing what time with Sam I could steal. "How did you meet?"

"You know, it was funny. I was absorbed in my assignments at school, and one day when I was walking back to my dorm room, he just…appeared. It was crazy. It was like he just leapt in from some other place and appeared in front of me. He looked at me as if he knew me, like he had been searching for me. I know it sounds funny, but it is true. He looked at me like he could see into my soul. I took one look at him and kind of got lost in his eyes. The rest is history."

"Oh," was all I said, wanting to hide my jealousy. Sure, I was glad Samantha was happy. She deserved some happiness in life after losing both of her parents to a drunk driver, but I wondered how I would fit into her new existence.

"I've missed you so much, Sam. I really missed our all-night chat fests." I waited to hear if she missed me also or if Don had completely replaced me in her life.

"That is exactly why I'm calling you. Don and I have purchased an old Victorian house just outside of town. It really needs a lot of work. I want the family to see the house and meet Don. I was hoping you could talk your mom and dad into driving out next Sunday. I want to show off my new husband, so I plan on calling all the other relatives and inviting them also. It will be a party to celebrate our marriage and our first house. Do you think you can get Uncle Jim and Aunt Mary to forgive me and come?"

"I can only try. They were pretty upset when you told them you eloped. I'm sure if I ever eloped they would never speak to me again. I really want to see you and meet Don, so…I will take on the wrath of hell and talk to them."

"Thank you so much. I knew I could count on you. Do you have a pen and paper?"

"Yes."

"Okay, write this down. You leave Somerset and take Main Street north to interstate 80. Go west, southwest on interstate 80. It will become Russell Springs Road. Follow Russell Springs—Wait, this is getting confusing. How about I email you the directions?"

"That would be perfect. You know Dad; he has to see it to drive it," I joked.

"There is something else."

"What?" I asked cautiously.

"I was also hoping you could stay the summer and help me set up the house.

What do you think?"

"Yes! Yes! I don't care if Mom and Dad say no. I'll talk them into it. I can't wait until I can spend some quality time with you."

She was offering me time with her and an alternative to the boredom of my summer vacation. Renovation on the old house would take all summer, and even though it meant I would be working every day of my vacation, at least Samantha and I would be together. I looked forward to this adventure.

I could never understand why my dad insisted on driving with the entire Baker army in one car. I would have preferred to drive my own car, but since I didn't have one I was forced to ride with the entire Baker clan in my family's old white utility van. It was more like a bus than a van. My father purchased the used extended van from a church because it could seat all of us. Being seen in this along with my many siblings was embarrassing at best. I was glad I was invisible.

After a cramped drive, my family and I arrived at the old Victorian. The house stood crested on the top of a hill. A circle drive escorted all visitors to the front double-door entrance. The house looked massive. It had at least three separate floors, and I imagined at least a dozen rooms on each. If I was going to stay here, I would surely have my own room. This would be the first time I had ever slept alone in my life, and the thought scared me. Wrapped in trepidation, self-absorbed, I waited with my family on the doorstep and rang the bell.

Sam opened the door, and I gasped in shock. Samantha was beautiful. Her hair shimmered with soft blond highlights. Her eyes glistened green like emeralds. She was confident, graceful, amazing, and...no longer invisible. We could never be confused for sisters again.

"Do you see a difference in Sam?" I asked my youngest sister, Katie.

"No, she looks like the same old Sam to me."

I pushed through the crowded family hellos to get to my mother.

"Does Sam look different to you?"

"She looks very happy."

"But her hair and eyes. You don't think she looks any different?"

"No. I don't know what your problem is, she looks just fine."

Was I the only one able to see this remarkable change in Samantha? After our hellos, Sam introduced us to Don.

He was every bit as handsome as Sam had described. He stood over six feet tall with blond hair almost the exact same shade as Sam's. His eyes were also the same brilliant emerald green.

Sam leaned into his arm, making the pair inseparable. It was obvious they were in love just by they way they looked at each other. Their love glowed around them like a halo. Maybe it was possible to actually see love like it was a color in a rainbow.

Sam proudly informed the family Don was a research scientist. He had purchased the old house as a wedding gift for her. She put her arms around my parents and towed them deeper into the house to show them around.

Don left us to answer the door and greet his next guests. I stared at my new brother-in-law. He looked older than Sam, maybe thirty. He seemed confident as he greeted his arriving guests. He had the manners of someone well educated and successful. Even though he defined confidence by his movements, his eyes never stopped scanning for Samantha. As soon as she re-entered the room, Don quickly took his place at her side. His arms were always around her waist, and his eyes were never off her. He worshipped her every movement. I have to admit I felt jealous and left out.

The party was noisy, and their house was soon packed with people. The family and friends invited poured through the floors, filling the spaces in the house like a flood. Sam swam through the maze of people with the skill of an Olympian. I admired her grace and beauty. *I could never look that amazing*, I thought. When she finally reached me, I was standing on a small balcony overseeing the sea of people.

"I want you to meet someone." She had to yell. I could barely hear her over the surrounding noise. "David" was all I could make out of her next sentence. She pointed into the crowd and beckoned to someone. A boy, no, a man moved at her command and began to make his way through the crowd to where we stood.

As he came closer I gasped. He was the most perfect male I had ever seen. I couldn't take my eyes off of him. He was tall and slender. The dress shirt he wore was opened at the collar, with sleeves rolled just below the elbow. His shirt clung to him, accentuating his muscular frame. His hair was blond and tousled, falling casually across his forehead. I wondered what it would feel like to run my fingers through his hair. His eyes were the most amazing shade of deep sapphire blue. He stared at me, and I was transfixed. He moved closer, standing just below the balcony were I stood, and then he extended his hand up to me.

I tried to breathe, but his eyes held me in a magical cocoon devoid of sound, movement or air. Everyone else in the room disappeared in that moment. In a trance, I held out my hand and my fingers touched his. In an instant, a shot of electricity ran though me. My pulse quickened, my heart pounded, my face flushed. In one move, he stood by my side still holding my hand.

Standing next to him, I became aware of the sharp contrast between us. I was acutely aware that any moment of awe was completely one sided. He was intrepid in his movements. He was older than me, maybe twenty. He was tall with Adonis's body. I stood a good foot below him in height. He was blond and blue eyed. I was insignificant in comparison.

I don't know if it was the difference in our heights or the fact the crowd was so noisy, but to my good fortune, he bent down to speak into my ear. I was glad he still held my hand. His nearness caused me to be unsteady on my feet.

"Hello, my name is David. I'm Don's brother. You must be Allyson. Sam wanted me to introduce myself. I'll be staying with them this summer to help with the renovation, so we will be seeing a good deal of one another."

With that announcement, he let go of my hand and walked back into the sea of people. I watched him drown in the crowd. He stopped only once, turning back to stare at me, and then disappeared.

I stood soldered in place. Of course he was Don's brother. I saw the obvious resemblance. Both were drop-dead perfect, but David was more compelling. I had never felt like this before. Meeting David was like looking fate in the face. David would be spending the entire summer close to me. Did I hear that part correctly or just imagine it? I knew whatever was meant to happen between David and I would remain out of my control, but I didn't care. I was going to enjoy every minute of this adventure.

After the party, I returned home with my family for the last week of my junior year in high school. Time seemed to stand still, filling me with even more anticipation. Finally the end of the week arrived, and my father drove me back to the old Victorian. Maybe it was because I was excited about being with Sam again or maybe it was just the incredibly slow way my father drove, but the drive took forever. We finally reached our destination just before sunset. My dad insisted on talking to Sam and Don for what seemed like an eternity. He was full of questions about inane subjects. I think he was hesitant to leave me there. I wished he would stop treating me like I was a baby. My father finally made his good-byes, handed Don my suitcase, kissed me, and left.

Don disappeared up the grand staircase with my bag, leaving me alone with Samantha.

"I better show you around the place so you don't get lost," she stated.

"This place is huge. It really needs a name like Grand View or Stately Manor," I joked.

"I like Stately Manor or Saltately Manor," Sam joked back, changing the new title to include her new last name.

We began our tour on the first floor. I was amazed at how large the house was. It didn't appear this big when I was here for the house-warming party. I reasoned the sea of guests hid the details of the house from me.

Saltately Manor greeted guests with a large entryway that opened into the living room. The living room sat on the right of the entry and was so massive it could have contained the first three rooms of the apartment I lived in. One entire wall was dedicated to housing the fireplace. The hearth alone was at least ten feet long and eight feet wide bigger than my bedroom. There was a leather chair and matching loveseat facing a flat-screen television on the adjacent wall. This was the only useful part of the parlor. Boxes haphazardly occupied the rest of the space.

Sam led me to two glass French doors filling the wall opposite of the fireplace. Sam pulled open the doors, and we entered the grand dining room. The space was filled with more boxes stacked against the walls. Only a crystal chandelier hanging from the center of the ceiling defined this space as the dining room and not a storage area.

We walked through a swinging door on the opposite wall and entered the kitchen. Maple cabinets wrapped around the entire perimeter, interrupted by gaping voids designated for the arrival of appliances. The room was anchored by a massive, dark-brown, granite-topped island in the center.

"I ordered bar stools for the island. They should be here in the next day or two, so we will eat in here until the dining room can be unpacked," Sam interjected.

There were maid's quarters just off the left side of the kitchen. Samantha explained her plans to convert this into the laundry room. We walked passed the room into a corridor where we were met by another smaller staircase circling upward. I craned my head back trying to see the top. "How far do they go up?" I asked.

"These stairs go up to the third floor. It is vacant. I don't think the original owners used it for anything more than storage. I don't know what we will do with that space. Rent it out, I suppose," she said laughing.

We followed the corridor past another room. Sam opened the door, and I peered in. A large walnut desk stood in front of the long paned window. Matching walnut shelves covered the walls. "Don is planning on making this room his office or library." Sam announced.

She closed the door, and we continued to follow the corridor until we arrived back at the entryway. Sam guided us up the grand staircase to the second level.

I hesitated on the balcony, turning to look down into the living room below. This was where I first met David. I remembered the sound of his voice in my ear, the touch of his hand on mine, and the sight of his perfect face before he disappeared into the crowd. Waking from my daydream, I realized Samantha had continued on her tour without me. I turned and scurried up the staircase to the second floor before she could notice my absence.

The second floor forked to the right and the left at the top of the stairs. We turned to walk the right side first. A fence of mahogany matching the stairs skirted the walkway. There was one massive mahogany door on this fork. This door opened to the master suite, Don and Sam's bedroom. There was a huge king-size bed, several dressers, and even a table and chair set up by the window. The windows led to a balcony overlooking the grounds of the estate. The master bedroom had a huge bathroom complete with his and hers sinks and ceiling-to-floor mirrors. The room was huge. The tub alone was more the size of a sunken pool than a bathtub. There was also a separate shower and sauna.

We exited the master suite and returned to the walkway, now passing to the left. More mahogany doors lined this corridor.

"The first room is yours. David will sleep in the room next door. I hope you don't mind," Sam said with a giggle.

She opened the door to my room. I peered into the darkened space. The light from the hall illuminated a single bed on the far wall under the only window. My suitcase stood waiting at the foot of the bed. The room was small compared to the master suite but about three times the size of the bedroom I shared with my sisters. This would be the first time in my life I would sleep alone.

Sam closed the door and continued her guided tour through the reminder of Saltately Manor. There were two more bedrooms and a bathroom at the end of the corridor. "You and David will be sharing this bathroom. You'll have to work out a schedule," Sam suggested.

Talking to David about the use of our bathroom would be embarrassing. At least I wouldn't have to worry about that conversation tonight. There was no sign of David, and I wondered when he would be moving in to Saltately Manor.

We turned at the end of the corridor and followed the walkway back to the staircase and down into the living room.

"I thought we could pop some popcorn and maybe watch a movie," Sam said as she glided into Don's waiting arms. They kissed briefly and Sam walked to the kitchen to get the popcorn, leaving me alone with Don.

"Do you mind what we watch?" Don asked me.

"No, anything is fine. You decide."

Don turned his attention to a brown box full of DVDs. "I think we will watch a…comedy." Don made his selection, pulled out a DVD, and placed it into the player.

Sam returned from the kitchen carrying a large bowl of popcorn and was followed by David.

"Look who I found," she said playfully.

Samantha sat on Don's lap as the two cuddled into the small arm chair. With no other place to sit, I apprehensively sat next to David on the love seat. I looked up to see Sam smiling like a Cheshire cat. I was certain she planned the move just to force me next to David.

I could not concentrate on the film. It must have been a good movie because the others were laughing and acting silly. I just sat there absorbed in my thoughts, silent. Sitting next to David was all I could think about. The warmth of his body and the scent of his skin were intoxicating. David must have noticed me deep in thought and threw a few pieces of popcorn at me.

"Come on, don't you think this is funny?" he said.

I forced a smile and made brief eye contact with him. When the movie was over, Sam got up and announced she and Don were going to bed. They would see us in the morning at breakfast. David stood up also, so I thought this was my cue to end the evening as well. Sam and Don turned and walked upstairs, and I dutifully began to follow. It was then David grabbed my arm.

"Let's let them have a few minutes to themselves. Newlyweds. You can help me lock up. Okay?"

I nodded. I would gladly stay up the entire night and walk to the edge of the world if it meant more time with him.

We began walking through the first floor of the house. David checked to make sure all the doors were locked and then instructed me to turn off the lights as we left each room. When the first floor was secure, he took my hand and led me up the stairs. The touch of his hand caused the blood to rush from my head, leaving me dizzy. The thought of our bedrooms being next to each other caused my heart to beat faster. I don't know what frightened me more, the thought of sleeping alone for the first time in my life or knowing David slept just a few feet away. My heart was pounding so loud I was sure he could hear it. He was still holding my hand when we reached the door to my room. I swallowed hard and waited for what came next. David opened the door for me. Holding firm to his hand as if it were my lifeline, I took a deep breath and apprehensively stepped in. He slipped his hand from mine and disappeared into his room, closing the door.

I was completely alone, and that reality washed me with fear. I would have to walk the length of the dark space to reach the lamp and my first hope of light. I walked cautiously, groping my way through the blackness to the night-stand on the far end of the room. Reaching the lamp, I turned it on. I survived the dimly light space. I decided I would have to make it through the night alone. It was time I grew up.

I picked up my suitcase from the floor where Don had left it, placed it on the bed, and began to unpack. I had no idea what the suitcase held. My mother had packed for me. She still saw me as a child even though I was sixteen. I was surprised at how many dressy tops, skirts, and shorts she had packed. Didn't she know I was here to work? I carefully arranged them into several outfits. It was then, to my horror, I found my only nightgown. Back home I always slept in one of my dad's old shirts. I would have been happy to have found one now, but my mother had packed one of her better silk nightgowns instead. It was black lace and nearly see-through. The strings tied at the shoulders barely were able to hold the weight of the floor-length lace. I didn't understand my mother. First I wasn't old enough to pack my own suitcase and next she gives me this nightmare from Victoria's Secret to wear. What was she thinking, packing this tool of seduction? Out of desperation and having nothing else to wear, I put it on.

I closed the suitcase and shoved it under the bed and looked around the room. The room contained the bed, nightstand, and a tall chest of drawers. I put some underwear, shorts, and tops in the dresser and looked around for a place to hang the dressier apparel. There was one other door in the room, and I assumed it to be the closet. I walk to the door, turned the handle, and opened it. I gasped. The door did not open to a closet. It was an adjoining door to…David's room. I stood in shock as David turned to mirror my expression. We stared at each other awkwardly.

His room was larger than mine. It held a double bed with a nightstand on either side. The door to the hall was closed so the only light came from the small lamps on the nightstands, giving the room a soft golden glow.

He wore only pajama bottoms, no shirt. A silver chain, hanging from his neck, glistened in the dim light of the room. An oval black stone hung from the chain, resting near his heart. Even in the diminished light I could see the perfect contour of his muscles. David was beautiful.

I could feel David's stare. I tried to swallow in an effort to snap myself back to reality. I had to find a way to make an exit and end the glaring way he looked at me. "I'm sorry. I thought it was the closet," was all I could say.

"So did I," he responded equally amazed.

"Well, good night," I said, trying to casually return to my room.

"You can leave the door open if it makes you feel safer," David answered.

"No, that's all right." I quickly ducked back into my own room, pushing the door closed. But at the last second, I stopped and left a small opening. I don't know why I left the door open. Was I really that afraid to sleep in a room alone or did I want to be nearer to him?

It was then I heard his soft laughter. The sound cut into me. Of course he thought I was some silly little girl. I was acting like one. Embarrassed, I jumped into my bed, turning out the light in one easy movement. I lay in the dark reliving the foolish way I had acted. What must he be thinking about me and how would I face him tomorrow?

Chapter 2

Rescue

I awoke the next morning deciding my best course of action was to avoid David as much as possible. Maybe he would forget me accidentally entering his room. With that in mind, I stayed in my room writing in my journal until all sounds of David moving about vanished. I then opened my door, checking to be sure my plan of avoidance worked, and quietly stole down the stairs to the kitchen.

I hesitated at the kitchen door and listened. I did not hear David's voice so I knew it was safe to enter. Samantha sat at the island drinking her morning coffee.

"Well, I'm glad *you* slept well," she teased. "Everyone has been up for at least an hour. Don and Dave went to pick up some building supplies. Coffee is ready. I would like to get started unpacking some of these boxes and making my new house into a home. Do you think you rested enough to help me?" She swatted at me, and I hit her back.

I was grateful to have something to do and an excuse to distance myself from David. I could just imagine what he must think of me. Sam directed as I explored a never-ending stream of boxes stacked throughout the house. Samantha oversaw the placement of each object, like general commanding troops for battle. Sam knew every item of her inventory. Money seemed to be no concern for Don, I thought. He seemed incapable of saying no to any request Sam made of him. If he only knew Sam's addiction to pretty things, he might have given her some restrictions, but she was allowed to go wild.

I spent the greater part of the next few days working alone, unpacking boxes and avoiding David. The unmarked boxes were filled with imported china, crystal, and silver. There were boxes of linens, towels, and brocaded blankets. Lamps, candles, electronics, anything a young homemaker could wish for, just seemed to appear. Don, I hypothesized, must be very rich or very much in love.

My work was monotonous. I sought a way to break the silence and questioned Samantha in hopes of starting up a conversation. "How did you meet Don?"

She took a deep breath and sighed. "My last year of college wasn't going very smoothly for me. My roommate barely talked to me. It wasn't that we disliked each other or anything like that. We were just two very different people who didn't share much in common. I have to admit I was homesick also and didn't make an effort to talk to her either.

"I wasn't doing well in my classes. No matter how hard I tried, I just couldn't pass biology. The professor I had was difficult to understand, and I think he also didn't like me very much. I had just finished my midterm exam and went to pick up my grade. Even though I had studied nonstop for the last three days, I flunked. I went to the professor to beg for a retest, but he wouldn't even give me the time of day. I couldn't flunk biology. It would affect my scholarship.

"I guess everything just came to a head then. While I was walking back to my dorm room, I started crying. I just couldn't stop. It was then I heard a voice from behind me say, 'A pretty girl like you shouldn't be crying. Can I help?' I turned around and saw Don. I don't know where he came from. It was like he just …appeared. One minute I was on the path alone and the next he was standing there. He stared at me like he could read my every thought, like he knew me. We started talking, and he walked me back to my dorm room. It felt comfortable to confide in him, and I forgot all about my biology grade. We must have spent half a day just talking. Then he asked to take me to dinner the next day, and I said yes. There was just something about him. Maybe it was his eyes or his voice, but I felt perfectly comfortable with him. We began seeing each other every day after that. He even went to my biology professor and talked him into giving me a retest. I became so dependent on Don, I couldn't see my life without him. He filled my every thought, and when he told me he couldn't picture his life without me either, I thought my heart would pound out of my chest. It was then he asked me to marry him. Without hesitating, I said yes and, well, you know the rest."

"Marriage must agree with you, Mrs. Saltate. You look amazing. Your hair and eyes just glow. It's like you are a different person from the Sam I grew up with. I don't think we could pass for sisters any more. You look beautiful."

"I feel beautiful, but that's all because of Don. It has nothing to do with me. I haven't changed. Don told me when you are truly in love, you glow from the inside out. Your soul becomes pure light, and you shine in your own personal halo. I don't know if it is true, but it sounded wonderful when he said it. I guess I found my soul mate.

"Maybe David can bring out the best in you," she said, pushing against me with her shoulder.

I blushed. Sam knew me too well. Of course she could see I thought David was amazing, but after the fiasco of the adjoining door, I was sure he thought I was just an irritant. I prayed she didn't have any matchmaking ideas on her mind. I would die of embarrassment if she forced David to notice me.

"Don't you think David is hot?" Sam gave me a sisterly shove and smiled.

"Sam!"

"Oh, I know he is my new brother, and I think Don is way sexier, but I do think you and David could make a cute couple."

"Leave it alone. He is tall and perfect, and I am short and, well, *me*. It is not a match made in heaven, and I would just die if he knew I liked him."

Sam just giggled deviously, and we went back to unpacking the boxes.

It was impossible to use the kitchen at the house except to make toast or pop popcorn. Don took charge and called a restaurant for dinner reservations. Sam took this outing as a chance to play matchmaker, much to my chagrin. She forced David into sharing the back seat of the car with me on the drive over and made sure we sat on the same side of the booth at the restaurant. It was humiliating.

The seating arrangements made it nearly impossible for me to swallow food. I could barely breathe just knowing he sat inches from me. I sat quietly, self-absorbed, and played with my meal in hopes of becoming invisible. The others gregariously chatted, but I paid no attention to them. Out of boredom, I began to look around at the other people in the restaurant.

Seated across from us was a young couple. He was tanned, buffed, and handsome with a date perfectly matching him. They would have made an amazing couple, but there was something dark and forbidding about them. They ate hardly speaking or looking at one another.

In contrast, the next booth over contained another young couple. They were very ordinary in their appearance but very enamored with one another. Maybe they weren't very attractive, but I could tell they honestly cared for each other. They glowed with love, as Sam said.

Samantha interrupted me from my wandering. "What's with you? There aren't enough hot guys at our booth; you have to check the restaurant for others?"

I blushed. "No," I answered quietly and returned to playing with my food.

"Ally Kat is going to be a writer. Did you know that, David? I bet if you asked her nicely, she would show you her diary. Wouldn't you, Ally Kat?" Samantha's taunting continued.

"Ally Kat?" David questioned, looking down at me.

"My name is Allyson Katherine," I explained. "My family shortened it to Ally Kat, and the nickname just stuck."

"That name doesn't suit you. You don't look like and alley cat. I'll just call you Allyson, if you don't mind."

"I don't mind," I replied. David could call me anything he wanted. Just the sound of his voice made whatever he said sound astounding.

"Let's play a game," Don said. "Tell me what you think the other people in the restaurant are talking about. We will start with the couple across from us. You go first, Allyson."

"I don't know. Can't someone else go first?"

"Come on, just say the first thing that comes into you mind," David said, nudging me with his arm.

"I think they are a handsome couple, but they don't look very happy with one another. There is darkness about him, selfishness. I think he is so much in love with himself, he doesn't care much about her and it is slowly draining the soul out of her." I looked up to see Don and David staring at me.

"What about the couple next to them?" David asked.

"I think they care very much about each other. They kind of have a sweet, romantic glow about them that makes them look…beautiful."

"Halo!" David spoke barely above a whisper.

I looked up and met his eyes staring back at me like I had said something amazing. I felt Don kick David under the table.

"Halo?" I questioned.

"No, I said hello. I agree with you," David quickly covered.

I lowered my eyes and returned to playing with my food. They continued to play the game with Samantha in the hot seat. All the time I could feel David staring at me. What had I said to upset him? After all, it was just a game.

I shadowed Samantha around Saltately Manor like a lost puppy for the next few days. It felt good to keep busy, but my thoughts were addictively about David. I couldn't get him out of my head and having him staring at me at every opportunity did not help.

I forced myself to only interact with David at meals. Even then, I sat focused on my plate, toying with my food. After dinner, we watched TV, and I made sure to sit on the floor, leaving the sofa entirely to David. Even though my contact with David was brief, I could still feel his constant stare. Whenever I glanced to look at him, his eyes were always waiting. My vivid imagination made up a host of explanations as to why he studied me so, but each explanation only nurtured my feelings of inadequacy.

My only solace was writing. I poured every thought and theory into my diary, but even with all my efforts, I couldn't get him out of my mind. I knew I could not keep this up forever.

"I cannot stand any more fast food or microwave junk." Don's booming announcement broke the silence of our breakfast one morning. "We are going shopping for some real food, Sam, and then I'm coming back and hooking up the stove. It is about time I find out if my new wife can cook.

Don then turned his attention to David. "Dave, I want you to start on the stove while Ally finishes setting up the cabinets." David shot a look at Don, passing some secret message between them. I could tell David was not happy about being left alone with me.

"Okay, my love, get dressed." Don left the kitchen with Sam dutifully following.

I stood up and began clearing the kitchen island of paper plates.

"It will be good to eat on china tonight," David said in an effort to make the best of our imposed togetherness. "I'll bring in the boxes from the garage, open them, and you put everything away."

"Some things should be washed first," I replied in an effort to keep the conversation going.

"I can help you with washing after everything is unpacked." With that David disappeared to the garage. He returned carrying two large brown boxes. We worked in silence except for some brief statements. Hours passed and the room began to take shape. The last task was to wash the dishes before putting them into the cabinets. Since the dishwasher had not been delivered, I offered to wash if David would dry, and he agreed. Standing side by side forced more awkward conversation.

"So, you want to be a writer. What kind of things do you like to write about?" David asked.

"I don't know. I tried poetry, but I wasn't very good at it. I've written a few short stories, and my English teachers said they were pretty good. I guess my dream is to write a novel some day."

"Have you written anything lately?"

"I'm working on something." I couldn't tell him every word I wrote was about him.

"Don't tell me. Let me guess. Mmm," he said, staring down at me.

I prayed I would not blush. His scrutiny was almost painful. I felt like he was trying to see into my soul and read my innermost thoughts.

"A romance novel," he said, looking at my face for a reaction. "I'm right, aren't I?"

The blush on my face answered before I could.

"I knew it. All teenage girls are consumed by romance."

The word "teenage" snapped me back to reality. I stood as tall and maturely as I could and defended my diary.

"The story I'm working on now is about an angel who travels through time to rescue a shy girl."

"Angel? Do you believe in angels?"

"I think people have souls and some people have such great souls they have to be angels."

"Can you tell who those people are? I mean, can you see if someone has a soul?"

"Everyone has a soul. As for being able to see someone's soul, I like to think I can see who is good and who is bad."

"Am I a good person? Do you think I have a soul?"

I wanted to say that I thought his soul was as beautiful as he was, but all I answered was, "Yes."

I finished washing the last dish and felt around under the suds to make sure the sink was empty. It was at that moment I ran my hand along something sharp. I let out a gasp and pulled my hand out of the water, staring at a cut running the length of my index finger.

David reacted by wrapping his fingers tightly over my hand pressing down in an effort to stop the bleeding.

Even in my daze, I could hear a car door close announcing Sam and Don's return. David relaxed his hold to check my finger, but it still gushed blood. His next attempt at first aid took me completely by surprise. He put my finger into his mouth. The feeling of his lips, the warmth of his mouth and the roughness of his tongue on my finger, made me swoon. He pulled my finger out to check only to be greeted by another pulse of blood.

"I think you need stitches. I better get you to Don." He wrapped his hand tightly around mine and pulled me into the closest bathroom. We could hear Don and Sam entering the house, and David shouted Don's name.

Don appeared at the bathroom door. "What's wrong?"

"Allyson cut her finger, and I can't stop the bleeding."

"How long ago?"

"Not long, just a few minutes. I think she needs stitches." David opened his hand to let Don examine my finger.

"It is not too bad, but I agree it needs to be sutured." Don left the bathroom and returned with a small medical bag.

"Wait! You're not a doctor," I exclaimed.

"Relax," David said, brushing back my hair with his other hand. "Don studied medicine before he decided to do research. You'll be okay." David placed his hand under my hair and gently caressed the back of my neck. He probably thought this would help calm me, but his touch had the opposite effect. My heart pounded wildly, and I gasped for breath. "Shh. I'm right here. I won't let anything hurt you. I'm your angel here to rescue you, remember?"

I couldn't bear him referring to himself as my "rescuing angel." *He must be having a good laugh at my expense*, I thought. With no way to escape, I turned my focus to Don.

Don first took a long, thin glass rod and touched it to my cut. A small amount of my blood eagerly flowed into it. I had seen my brother get stitches, and the doctors never took a blood sample before. "Why did you do that?" I questioned.

"I was just checking the wound to make sure there was nothing in it like broken glass."

"I cut myself on a knife."

"I'll be done in a few minutes. Just relax."

David knelt before me softly stroking my neck. I couldn't help but stare into his incredibly blue eyes. I couldn't feel anything other than his touch.

"Okay, all done and good as new," Don announced.

I looked at my hand to see my finger already bandaged. Don cleaned up and left the bathroom to us.

"Your hand is covered in my blood," I said.

"It will wash off. Are you okay?"

"Yes, I'm fine. I feel a little silly. I'm such a dork."

"Accidents happen. Don't be so hard on yourself." David slid his hand free of my neck and walk to the sink to wash. This was my cue to leave, but David called be back.

"Aren't you forgetting something?"

"What?"

"Don't you need a kiss to make it better?"

What kind of a kiss did he mean? Trembling, I held out my injured hand. David cupped it gently in his, kissing my finger…my palm…the back of my wrist … and then he softly pressed his lips to mine. Our eyes met and he smiled, turned, and walked away.

I stood frozen in the moment. Why was David acting so sweet? I was sure it wasn't because he was attracted to me. I rationalized he just enjoyed seeing defenseless girls swoon. I was no more than someone to practice his seduction techniques on. He couldn't really feel an attraction to me.

Chapter 3

Interlude

David and I woke each day at about the same time. Having to share one bathroom at home taught me to be quick. I was in and out in a few minutes. David took his time. It wasn't waiting for my turn that upset me; it was the numerous occasions he emerged wearing nothing but a towel precariously tied at his hips. I truly believed he enjoyed my reaction. I blushed a bright red and gasped most of the time. He would just laugh and squeeze past me.

I woke at sunrise, seizing the opportunity to beat him to the shower. I quietly slipped from my room and scurried to the bathroom. I showered quickly, dressed, and opened the door. David blocked the entrance.

"Good morning. I see you beat me to the shower."

"It is all yours." I tried to walk past him, but he blocked me, slowly circling. I stared into the onyx crystal he always wore around his neck. Maybe if I concentrated on the crystal I wouldn't blush at his close proximity.

"Sam and Don left a note. They're going to town, shopping. I swear Sam is going to break the guy. Anyway, we're alone."

What was I supposed to do with the announcement of "we're alone"? Just to be safe, I decided to ignore the comment.

"Sam likes nice things. She didn't have very much growing up with my family. This shopping thing is new to her. Your brother should just take charge and just say no once in awhile."

"It is very difficult to say no to the Baker girls."

I blushed, looked up, and met his eyes looking down at me.

He smiled and commanded, "Wait for me. We can have breakfast together."

"If you let me pass, I could have breakfast waiting on the table for you."

"Yes, my lady," he said with a bow. "See I told you it was impossible to say no to a Baker girl." He winked and let me pass.

I hurried downstairs to the kitchen. I put on the coffee and set the table for two. I was pouring a glass of orange juice when David entered the kitchen. He sat down while I returned to the eggs I was scrambling. I heard the toast pop up from the toaster and instinctively reached for it. David must have had the same reaction and our hands met. I pulled my hand away and returned to preparing the eggs.

David said, "I've got the toast. Would you like me to butter yours and put jam on it?"

"No, I can take care of it myself, thank you."

With the eggs completed, I turned to serve them. I noticed David had re-arranged the table setting so we sat next to each other. I sat down beside him as if I were indifferent to the new sitting arrangement.

"Tell me about you family," David began.

"What did you want to know?"

"Everything. Don and I only have each other. We never really knew our parents, so having a big family like yours interests me."

"Believe me, having an army of siblings is no picnic. You are lucky you just have Don."

"Still, I want to know all about the Bakers…and you."

Why in the world would David want to know about my family, or me for that matter? There was honesty in his eyes, so I resigned myself to answering his questions.

"My dad and mom met in high school. They got married as soon as they graduated. My dad served a few years in the Navy and my mom lived on base. My dad still runs the family like he is on a ship.

There are seven of us: John, Charlie, Robert, James, Karen, Katie, and me."

"Where do you fit in this line of Bakers?"

"I was the third child born and the oldest girl. My sisters are the youngest in the family, so I didn't have another girl to talk to until Samantha moved in."

"When was that?"

"My Uncle John and his wife died in a car accident when I was six. I don't remember much about them. It was after the accident Sam came to live with us. We have been sisters ever since."

"Describe Samantha to me."

"What?"

"You want to be a writer, describe Samantha to me."

I shook my head. I couldn't understand the reason for David's request.

"Samantha is a beautiful soul. She is generous, a good listener, and my sister. She shines from the inside out. Her beauty is as timeless as the sparkles in her emerald eyes. She will always be an important part of my life."

I looked up to see David studying me. It made me feel uncomfortable. I felt like he was trying to peer into the deepest part of my soul.

"Now describe me."

"I really don't want to."

"Please. You did such a great job on Sam. I'll make it easier. Close you eyes and try to describe what I'm wearing."

His clothes were easier to think about, but I still couldn't understand what he wanted from me. Was he continuing this charade for his own amusement?.

I closed my eyes and took a deep breath. I hoped I could generically describe him without the flush of pink coming to my cheeks.

"You are tall, about six feet two inches. You are wearing a pair of worn jeans hung on you hips because you never wear a belt. You have on an old blue dress shirt opened almost to your waist. I think you are very proud of your hairy chest because you show it off so much. You have a silver chain around your neck and a black crystal hangs from it. You never take the crystal off, so it must be very important to you."

I opened my eyes, pleased with myself for checking my emotions. Any control on my part vanished when I looked up to see him staring back.

"That is a physical description of me," he said staring. "But how do you feel about me?"

The question I dreaded. I wanted to answer; "I have never desired anyone like I desire you. I want to crawl inside you and get lost." I knew I couldn't leave myself vulnerable to a possible rebuff, so instead I said, "I think you are very self-confident. You know you are handsome, and you like to see how many women you can attract." I should have ended it with that, but there was something in his eyes that compelled me so I added, "I think you have a deeper purpose, some goal you need to achieve. I don't know what it is, but I feel something important drives you, like you're searching for a valuable prize."

I stopped and looked away from him. I felt I had said too much and waited for him to laugh. I was not prepared for his reaction.

"My God, you are amazing." He reached and took hold of my hand. I looked up to see him smiling. He had smiled at me before, but this time it felt different. It felt like we were connected in some way.

Samantha and Don returned from their shopping excursion carrying a large oil painting and two glass platters matching her set of china. It was amazing Sam could find anything left to purchase for Saltately Manor. I listened intently as Sam excitedly described each item captured on her latest hunting expedition.

David directed his attention to his brother. "Don, I need to talk to you. Can we go to your study?" Don led the way with David following. I'm sure David used "talking" as an excuse to rescue Don from rehashing the day's shopping trip. They seemed dependent on one another, like they were on some type of a mission where success was only assured if they had each others' backs.

I followed Sam into the living room.

"Do you think this painting looks better on this wall, above the fireplace, or maybe I should put it somewhere else in the house?"

"I think it would look fine above the mantle. You really don't have any of those colors in any other room. You could really play it up if you added some throw pillows or candles."

I knew I shouldn't have made that suggestion by Sam's delighted reaction: "Good, an excuse for another shopping trip."

"Sam, you really need to take it easy. You are going to drive Don into bankruptcy before your first wedding anniversary."

"I know I'm being silly, but Don said he and his family are very wealthy and it would be awhile before I could use up all their money."

"I'm sure he told you that before he knew how well you could shop."

Sam laughed. "Could you unpack the two platters and put them in the china cabinet? I was very lucky to find them. My pattern of china is already discontinued."

"I'll say you are lucky. You most likely own every piece ever made of this pattern and the manufacturer decided to quit while they were ahead."

I opened the box and took out the platters. Try as I would, I couldn't fit them into the buffet. I gave up and said, "They don't fit. Any other suggestions?"

"Try the kitchen. I'm going to try the painting in our bedroom." With that, Sam ran up the stairs.

I walked back into the kitchen and surveyed the cabinets. The shelves were stocked full. There was only one place the platters could possibly be stored — the cabinet above the refrigerator—but it was vertically beyond my reach. I didn't let the distance deter me. I placed the platters on the counter, pulled myself up onto the counter, and then lifted the platters to the top of the refrigerator, climbing into position after it. It was at that moment David came back into the kitchen.

He looked up, startled by my precarious perch.

"What are you doing? Come down from there before you fall."

"I know what I'm doing. I do this all the time at home."

"Well you are not doing it here." He stretched up his arms to try to help me down. Even though he was over six feet tall, the angled distance between us was about three feet. I hesitated to move. "Come on" he ordered again. I pushed myself off with my feet to be sure I cleared the distance. The thrust was more than David expected, and we fell to the floor. I heard his head hit. Stunned, we both lay motionless with the weight of my body pressing down against him. Staring into his eyes, I wove my arms around his neck and ran my fingers through the hair on the back of his head. I rationalized I needed to check for the possibility of blood, but the real reason was I wanted to embrace him and pull my body even closer to his.

He continued to look deeply into my eyes. I couldn't move.

"Are you okay?" I questioned.

"I'm fine. Are you?"

"I'm alright, but I'm not the one who hit his head." I tried to get up off of him, but he wrapped his arms around my waist, pulling me even closer to him.

"This is comfortable. Don't move just yet," David said.

I relaxed and let the weight of my body conform to every curve and bend of his. It was amazing how well our bodies fit together. I softly moved my fingers in his hair, letting his blond ringlets curled around my fingers in golden rings. I wanted to stay like this until I memorized his face, the feel of his arms around me, and his scent. I could feel his heart beating in time with mine.

The black crystal he always wore lay next to his head. There was a little speck of reflective light flashing a band of white across the center of the crystal. It made the stone appear like an eye watching me. In a trance I said, "It's so beautiful. I've never seen a stone like it. What is it called?" I began to unwind by left arm free and moved to touch the crystal.

"Don't touch it!" David commanded, breaking the mood. I froze. He ran his hands down the sides of my body, pressing into each side of my waist, and lifted me up. With one swift movement, he rolled me to my back and pressed his body down on mine. I took a deep breath and wove my fingers more tightly into his hair. David gazed down hungrily at me. I was completely under his spell. I closed my eyes, waiting for his next move, but he quickly rolled away, stood, and left the kitchen. I lay on the cold floor more confused than ever. I had felt something magical happen between us. Did he feel something too?

Chapter 4

Thunder

The summer was coming to an end, along with my proximity to David. I was hopelessly drawn to him. I couldn't bear the thought of not seeing him every day. My only solace was recording my feelings in the book I now worked on. I recorded every imagined encounter. I was the heroine and David most certainly was the hero. I imagined David professing his love to me, and the two of us would go off into the sunset. It was a beautiful ending to my story, but I knew in my heart it was just a fantasy.

I kept my journal carefully hidden, unlike my feelings for David. I watched his every move. I hung on each word he uttered. I tried to memorize everything about him because I knew, in less than two weeks, I would be back home and back to the reality that was my life.

David seemed comfortable around me, but he was hardly infatuated with me. He acted more like a protective big brother than boyfriend material. He was always kind and courteous but distant. I sometimes felt he thought I was some kind of piece of fine crystal he was assigned to guard. If I had any hope of David seeing me as anything other than a little girl, our next encounter would set me straight.

The night started out like any other August night. The heat of the day moaned out of the burned earth, making the evening air even heavier. The clouds hung low in the sky, blocking out the moon, and then a thunderstorm began. I had always been terrified of thunder and lightning. When I was little, my grandmother came to stay with us. Each time a thunderstorm erupted, it prompted her to retell the story of lightning striking her family's home. They narrowly escaped with their lives and stood helplessly watching as their house burned to the ground. Her vivid description of the event terrified me as a child. I could imagine the cries of my grandmother's family and feel their fear as they fought to escape the flames raging around them. I felt the pain of being unable to save all your memories, hopes, and dreams.

Perhaps that is why I always spent stormy nights in my parents' room. But what would I do now? There were no parents to run to. I couldn't run to Don and Sam. They slept on the other side of the house; besides, I couldn't disturb them. David slept just a few feet away, through an unlocked adjoining door. I thought about calling to him for help, but it would surely seal my fate. He could never see me as anything other than a little girl if I acted like one now. I pressed my head into my pillow to block the sound of the storm.

The storm intensified. Each spark of light illuminated my fear. Each clap of thunder slapped me to my very core. I had to do something. Finally, out of desperation, I walked to the adjoining door. I opened it and walked into David's room.

David slept soundly, unaware of the storm raging outside.

I looked down, hesitant to move, but the next flash of lightning pushed me closer to him out of desperation. I looked down at his calm, shirtless body. He looked more like a statue, too perfect to be real. I called his name softly, but he didn't respond. With trembling fingers, I touched his shoulder and called once more, "David."

Startled by my touch, he opened his eyes.

My fear of the storm was greater than the humiliation I risked. I realized my next move would change our relationship forever. All I could manage to choke out was, "Help me."

Without a word, he pulled back the covers and I fell into his waiting arms. I don't know if it was my fear of the storm or the fact that I was acting like such a baby, but I began to cry. He pulled the blanket over us, wrapping me in the warmth of his embrace. My head fit perfectly against his shoulder. My body warmed as it stretched the length of his. He softly brushed my hair back and consolingly said, "Shh." I cuddled closer.

He whispered in my ear, "You're okay. I won't let anything hurt you." The sound of his voice caused my body to tremble. He must have thought I was cold and pulled me closer to him. I jumped with each thunderclap. I quivered with each burst of lightning. David never let go. He was protective, com-forting, and I dare say, loving. I continued to cry until I finally cried myself to sleep. My dreams were of David as I slept soundly in his arms.

The light of dawn slowly pulled me to consciousness. Still dreaming, I stretched out my arm to feel the curve of my pillow. But my fingers ran over soft chest hair instead of linen. Confused by this new sensation, I opened my eyes to David staring back at me. I moved my arm, pulling across his chest, but David grabbed my wrist and pulled my arm off of him. The suddenness of his movement jolted me to a sitting position on the edge of his bed.

David coldly looked at me. "It's morning. You better go back to your own room before Sam and Don wake up."

His tone splashed over me like cold water. It didn't take a genius to know David was finished being my protector. He wanted me out of his room. I stepped out of his bed and walked to the door, but something held me in place. I felt I just couldn't leave after exposing so much of myself. I had to say something.

The morning sun was burning through the window in my room. The light framed me from behind, blazing around me like my personal halo. I turned to look back and saw David sitting in bed, transfixed. The morning light in his face made his eyes burn with blue fire. I swallowed and shyly said, "Thank you."

"Just, *please,* go back to your room and close the door," he said curtly.

Rejected, I stepped into my room, closing the door as instructed. I turned the lock, sealing the separation between us.

My action the night before had sealed my fate. I *was* a little girl, and he was tired of babysitting me. Heartbroken, I poured my pain into my journal. The pain of losing all hope of being David's consumed me.

Chapter 5

Leaving

I had two more weeks until I would leave for home, two more excruciatingly long weeks. I stayed to myself, writing in my journal. It felt familiar to be invisible again.

It was easy to avoid David. He seemed to be avoiding me. I never had to beat him to the morning shower. He was always up and gone when I awoke. Whenever I entered a room, he would leave. He went out almost every night and did not have dinner with us. He always came in late after I was in bed.

There wasn't anything left to clean, sort, or repair at Saltately Manor. I spent every day trying to avoid the crushing heat of August outside while enduring David's ice-cold avoidance inside. I spent most of my time writing. It helped to record my every thought and feeling. I needed some type of a release before I snapped from the extremes of my existence. I longed for my silent imprisonment to be over.

One evening, David actually joined us for dinner. I hoped he had forgotten the night of the storm. We sat across from each other at the table, but David made no eye contact with me. Even though we all engaged in useless conversation, David did not speak to anyone but Don. Even then, his conversation sounded curt and restricted. It was like the two brothers spoke in a code of innuendos only they could understand.

When we were finished eating, Sam, Don, and David walked into the living room. I feared David might stay at home tonight, so I busied myself washing dishes. At least cleaning the kitchen would give me a reason to stay away from the three of them. I took my time, and when I couldn't drag it out any longer, I shut off the light and joined them.

Sam was curled up in Don's arms. The pair of lovebirds stretched out on the couch, engrossed in some documentary on TV. David sat on the only other chair. I hesitated for a moment. Should I stay or go to my room? I decided to stay and moved to sit on the floor.

"Here, take my chair. I was just leaving." David stood and walked out the front door. The cold slam made my chest twist. I sat in the leather chair abandoned by David. If I had hoped to control my feelings for him, sitting here didn't help. The chair wrapped me up in everything David. The leather still held the warmth of his body, the shape of his form, and the scent of his skin. I let myself be cocooned in its essences. I surrendered to my feelings and thoughts. I would always desire David, but those feeling would never be returned.

Lost in my own world, I had not noticed the documentary ending. Don got up and turned off the TV, cueing me it was time to go to bed. Sam and I began to head upstairs while Don turned off the lights in the parlor. We were interrupted by a knock on the front door. Don, being the closest, opened it. Standing on the other side was a beautiful, tall, chestnut-haired girl. Her arms were around a slumped over figure I assumed to be David. I recognized the blond top of his head. His body leaned against the tall, beautiful girl as she supported his weight with the full length of her body. She held David's waist in both her arms, and he rested his head against her shoulder.

"Are you Don Saltate?" she inquired.

"Yes"

"My name is Mandy. I'm the bartender at Pete's just up the road. Your brother was in our place tonight, and I think he had a little too much to drink, so I brought him home. Here are the keys for his car." She reached forward to pass the keys to Don. "I would like you to call me a cab so I can get back to Pete's; and under the circumstances, I also think you should pay for it, don't you?"

Don reached out, effortlessly pulling David to a staggered standing position.

"Thank you. I'll take him from here."

Sam walked down the stairs to the door. "Hi, I'm Samantha, David's sister-in-law. Thank you so very much for looking out for our David. I would be happy to drive you back to your car."

Sam grabbed the car keys from Don and left with the chestnut-haired beauty, pulling the door closed behind her.

"David!" Don shouted, but David did not respond. "Look at me! What were you thinking, going out and getting drunk? You know better than that. What if you just started telling everything to everybody? Where would we be?"

David opened his eyes and looked at Don. "I can't take it any more. I can't do it. She is so sweet and innocent. Did you see how sweet she is? I can't do it. I can't take her back or forward. It just isn't right."

"Why do you think I decided to stay here? I told you, *nothing* has to be decided now. Just give it time." Don helped David walk upstairs to his bedroom. I followed behind silently observing.

David continued to mumble, "A few days, a week, a year, it still would not be right. I want to protect her. She is too valuable to be left alone, but the closer I get, the more I risk hurting her. How do I protect her from me?"

They walked into David's room, and Don dumped David onto the bed. "Okay, we will talk about this in the morning. You've said enough already. Let's get you comfortable so you can sleep it off."

Don must have remembered I was still standing in the hall. He turned to me and said, "I'm going to need your help." I walked into the room and stood by the side of the bed.

David began muttering again. "Maybe I should leave. At least then I wouldn't be tempted all the time. She is just so beautiful... Don't you think she is beautiful?" David waved his arm trying to grab Don and his attention, but his movements were uncoordinated.

"Yes, yes. Now try to settle down and get some sleep."

David must not have known I was in the room. He continued to speak incoherently. "I can't. She's always right there. She is stuck in my head. I can't get myself out from under her halo... Don't you think she has a powerful halo? And beautiful. I want her, God help me. She fits into my arms and against my body as if we were made to be together...She trusts me...How can I tell her she is just an experiment?"

"You talk too much. Try to fall asleep."

Don tried to make David more comfortable. He pulled the blanket back on the bed and pushed a pillow under David's head. Don looked at me, commanding, "Unbutton his shirt while I get his shoes and pants off."

David kept muttering in slurred speech, and then he looked around the room as if he were searching for something. "I hate this room. I hate this house. She is in every inch of it. I can't go anywhere where I can't feel her. She fills my mind. It is like she has me wrapped in her halo. I can't get her out of my mind... Did I tell you I slept with her, Don?"

"You what!"

"I slept with her. Right here in this bed... She felt amazing."

"Tell me I didn't hear you correctly. You slept with her?"

"Yes. But not like that. I had to protect her. I had to take care of her. I have to... I have to... I have to get some sleep." David closed his eyes and lay still on his bed.

I continued to unbutton David's shirt completely. He opened his eyes, looking at me like he was trying to remember who I was. He just stared at me. I let go of his shirt and stood up, staring back. I could feel my heart pounding, so I turned my focus back to his shirt. David glanced down to watch the movement of my hands unbuttoning his shirt and exposing his bare chest. He looked back into my eyes and then yelled, "GET OUT! GET OUT!"

I stood in shock at the sound of David's scream. I couldn't believe what I was hearing. David began pushing me away. It was very clear to me he wanted me as far away from him as humanly possible.

"You can go. I can handle it from here," Don said, ignoring David's violent outburst.

I backed out of the room, turned, and ran to my room, shutting the door behind me. But even with the door to my room sealing me in, the sound of the brothers talking filtered through. David was telling Don everything was my fault. David blamed me.

What was I thinking? I had fantasized this Cinderella fairytale with him as the prince and me as the fair young maiden of his dreams. In reality, everything was just a figment of my imagination. It was like I was lost in one of my own stories. The reality was David wanted nothing to do with me. He had found the perfect girl, and it wasn't me. It was most likely that chestnut-haired beauty who brought him home. He wanted her, not me. He wanted me… out of his life. He had made his feelings about me clear. I decided, then and there, I was going home tomorrow, back to where I belonged.

I thought the night would never end. I hardly slept. The sound of David's mutterings kept me awake. I didn't even try to make out any of the words he said. I didn't want to hear any more than I had already.

I lay in bed very still and watched as the sunlight danced the morning across the floor of my room. I had promised myself I would not move until I heard Sam go down for breakfast. My plan was to hurry downstairs after her and convince her to take me home—today.

My reprieve finally arrived. I heard Don and Sam softly talking as they made their way down the staircase and to the kitchen. This was my opportunity to ask them to take me home. I jumped out of my bed, brushed the wrinkles out of the clothes I slept in, quietly turned the handle to open my door, and stepped out into the hallway. I had to move quickly for fear running into David. I stopped in the hall for a moment, straining to hear any noise coming from David's room, but there was nothing. Taking my chance, I scurried down the staircase.

I greeted Sam and Don good morning as they sat at the breakfast table. I began thanking them for having me and then quickly added my request that they take me home as soon as possible. This announcement took Sam by surprise. Why did I wish to leave with more than a week left of the summer? I lied and said I was homesick, and I think she believed me. Sam said she would try to find some time to drive me, but she had made several appointments for that day. Don had a meeting to attend at work. I begged and pleaded until they promised they would work it out. Victorious, I headed back upstairs to pack.

I closed my door when I got to my room. It was perfect timing. I heard David open his door and head downstairs. My curiosity got the better of me, and I snuck back down to a few stairs to eavesdrop.

David spoke first upon entering the kitchen. "Good morning. Where is everyone?"

"Well, I'm here, Don is in the den, Ally is packing, and you are in pain."

"Very funny, Sam."

"I have just what you need: a nice cup of black coffee."

"God bless you… Did I hear you correctly? Ally is packing?"

"Seems someone yelled at her last night and blamed her for his drinking. At least, that's what Don told me. Now she wants to go home. She claims she is homesick, but I think you hurt her feelings. I don't blame her. Don said you were pretty obnoxious last night. I don't know how Don and I can find the time today to drive her home."

"Where's Don?"

"In the den. Why?"

"I have to talk to him."

I heard David get up and walk to the den. I moved up a stair so he wouldn't see me. When he got to the den door, he said, "Don, I have to talk to you."

"Can we make it short? I have a meeting to attend; and then, thanks to you, I somehow have to make it back in time to take Ally home. I told you, you had time to decide what to do, but, no, you had to go get drunk, shoot you mouth off, and traumatize the poor girl."

"I have a problem, Don."

"David, you always have some problem or high drama in your life. I think it is time to grow up and start taking your responsibilities seriously. You know why we came here and what we have to do. I have made peace with it. Samantha is everything to me. Either you make peace with it or forget it and leave. So, what is your problem?"

"I think I'm in love."

"You are *always* in love, Dave."

"No. This time, it is different." With that said, someone closed the door to the den and I could not hear anything more.

I went back to my room, lost in my thoughts. Of course David was in love. The model that brought him home last night was amazing. At five feet ten with an unbelievable figure, what was not to love? It would explain why David had been going out so much in the last few weeks, but something must have happened between them causing David to drink last night. Maybe she wasn't as in love with him. What else could it be?

Time passed and there was a knock at my door. *Finally*, I thought, *Sam is here to rescue me and take me home*. I grabbed my suitcase, rushed to the door, and opened it. It wasn't Samantha. It was David.

He smiled at me and said, "Don said you wanted to be driven home. Since they are busy, I volunteered."

Great. More time alone with someone who hated me. I tried to step past him, but he stopped me. He put his hand on mine, trying to get me to release my hold of my suitcase. I resisted. I didn't want to be any more of a nuisance to him.

"Let go," he commanded.

"I can carry it."

"Let go."

I did as I was told. I walked down the stairs, opened the front door, and walked to David's car. I stayed as close to the door as possible, avoiding any contact. He put my suitcase in the back seat of his convertible and went around to the other side to get in.

We didn't speak to each other the entire drive. He didn't even turn on the radio. He just drove and stared straight ahead. As we got closer, I instructed him to pull over a few houses away. I didn't want David dropping me off in front of my house. I would die of embarrassment if my brothers saw me with him and began their usual teasing.

He pulled to the curb and stopped the car. This was my cue to step out. I opened the door, stepped onto the sidewalk, and, looking down at the ground to avoid eye contact, I mumbled, "Thank you." I reached into the back seat to retrieve my suitcase, but he put his hand on top of mine, preventing me from lifting it up.

"When am I going to see you again?" he asked softly.

I was shocked at his question. I looked up to see his amazing blue eyes staring back. "I don't know," was all I could say.

"That is not good enough. Can I see you tonight?"

I nodded yes in disbelief. Why was he doing this? Was he trying to have a good laugh at my expense? I tried to lift my suitcase, but his hand held firm.

"When?" he asked.

"I don't know."

"Six? Seven? Eight? Pick a time."

"Seven," was all I could think to say. I tried to lift my suitcase, but he would not let go of my hand.

"Where can I meet you?"

I knew I had to say something if I hoped for any escape from his grasp. "Right here, at seven." With that said, he let go of my hand. I turned and ran to the house as quickly as possible.

I didn't look back. I couldn't. I knew David must be teasing, and I didn't want my last image of him to be of him laughing at my expense. I knew I would never see him again. The thought tore through my heart and into my soul.

Chapter 6

Explanation

It felt good to be home and invisible again. No one seemed to notice my arrival a week early. The family went about their individual activities taking no notice of me walking through the apartment and into my room.

I locked the door of my bedroom and began to unpack. Everything I touched reminded me of David. I had to put him out of my mind. He wasn't part of my life and would never be. Yet, I couldn't understand why he asked to see me again. After much pondering, I decided seeing me was probably his last attempt to put me in my place. It would serve me right if I really believed he would be waiting for me tonight. I was certain his request was just a ploy to stand me up. I decided I wasn't going to fall for it.

I busied myself with dinner preparations, first cooking the meal and then setting the table. I sat quietly self-absorbed during dinner, letting everyone chatter back and forth. After dinner, I cleared the table, packaged the leftovers, and washed the dishes. After the last dish was in its place, I looked around the apartment. Some of my family watched television in the living room. Some went to their rooms to listen to music or play a game. Still other members of my family poured into the backyard to converse loudly. Wanting to be alone, I decided to go for a walk.

I quietly exited the apartment through the front door, stealing down the hallway staircase to the bottom door. I reached to turn the handle, but a shadowy movement on the other side of the frosted-glass door took me by surprise. With great trepidation, I turned the knob, slowly opened the door, and peered around it. There stood David, much to my amazement.

"I was beginning to think you forgot about me. It is almost seven-thirty."

David looked concerned. He studied my reaction for a moment and added, "You look surprised to see me."

"I am. I didn't think you'd actually show up."

"Why?"

"Well, last night… you wanted me out of your life."

"No, you misunderstood. Can we go somewhere we can talk? I have a great deal to explain to you, and this vestibule isn't very private."

"I was just going out for a walk."

"A walk it is." He took my hand and pulled me out the door. "Which way?"

"I usually just walk around the block," I replied, still amazed by his presence.

"Too busy. We need to be alone. Let's walk away from your house."

He pulled me across the busy street that ran in front of the apartment building. I had to run to keep up with his strides. We walked a block or more away from my home down a vacant side street of the city. On the corner of the block stood an old church. I knew once we were next to it the massive structure would block me from the sight of my family. I tightened my hand against his and waited for him to tell me what he really wanted.

When we reached the side of the church, David stopped and pushed me against the side of the church, taking me by surprise. I prepared myself for a confrontation. He leaned against me, staring down with those incredible blue eyes of his. I stared back and braced myself for his next move.

He placed his hand on the side of my face, softly caressing my cheek, fingering his way to the back of my neck. I took a deep breath and closed my eyes. He wrapped his fingers around the long braid of hair running the length of my back and pulled gently down on the braid, forcing my head to tilt upward to his, and kissed me. This kiss wasn't casual. This kiss was different. It felt hungry. He playfully sucked my upper lip into his mouth and then repeated the same motion on my bottom lip. I was unable to move. The blood rushed from my head to my heart. My leg buckled, giving out from under me. I would have fallen, but David arms held me firmly to him. When I finally opened my eyes, he was looking at me and smiling.

He released my hair and ran his hand down the side of my body gently taking my hand and resuming our walk.

I followed in a daze. If he was trying to drive me crazy, he succeeded. I was completely confused.

"Why are you being so nice to me?" I asked once I was able to breathe normally.

"Aren't I always nice to you?"

"Not *this* nice."

"I decided to stop fighting."

"Fighting with me?"

"No, fighting with the way I feel."

"Oh, David, I'm so confused. Sometime I feel you are speaking in riddles, and I just don't get it."

"Forgive me. I've never been in love before."

"Well if that girl means so much to you, why are you kissing me?"

"What girl?"

"The gorgeous model that made you drunk last night."

"You think I'm in love with the bartender?"

"She is beautiful. I can see why you would want her." I didn't realize how much it hurt to say it out loud. I put my head down in an effort to be invisible again.

David stopped walking and gently took my face in his hands. He weaved his head back and forth until I was forced to look into his eyes.

"I'm not in love with her. I'm in love with you."

I couldn't believe what I was hearing. "How is that possible? I mean… look at you. You are perfect, and I… well, I'm just forgettable me."

"You are far from forgettable. I've never met anyone like you." David must have seen the confusion still on my face and continued, "Do you remember the night of the storm?"

"Oh God, I'm so sorry about the way I acted. This is so embarrassing. You must think I'm some kind of an idiot to be frightened by a storm at my age."

"No, I don't think you are an idiot. Something happened that night." He brushed back a wisp of my hair with his hand. "You touched me."

David continued with his explanation. "You have to first understand who *I* am. Don and I grew up never knowing our parents. Where we come from, people don't care much for other people. Our parents didn't care about us and abandoned us to be raised by strangers in an orphanage. Even though we were left at the same facility, I did not meet Don until I was six and he was thirteen. When we first met, Don didn't really care about me. But we only had each other, so we were forced to become close. When it was time for Don to leave, he took me with him. We learned to rely on each other for everything, but something was still missing: our souls. Then Don came here and met Samantha. I saw how much she transformed him. For the first time, Don was… alive. I have to admit I was a little jealous of what they had. I didn't think I could ever find anyone who would make me feel alive, and then I met you. You took me completely by surprise."

"How?"

"You saw things differently. Remember the couples at the restaurant?"

I nodded yes.

"You could *see* into them, to their souls. You gave me hope that maybe you might be able to see into me, to see if I had a soul. I always believed I was born without one, causing me to always feel a void in my existence."

"Everyone has a soul," I said.

"Maybe not, but if anyone could find mine, I believed it to be you. I got closer to you, wanting to know you better. At first I was just curious. I thought I was in control of my feelings, that there was no way you could affect me. But the night of the storm… everything changed. I saw you differently. You were not just Sam's little cousin anymore. Holding you in my arms, I could feel my soul. You touched me to my very core. I wasn't prepared for it. After that night, I couldn't get enough of you and that feeling you gave me every time I was close to you. Did you know that most nights I opened the adjoining door just to watch you sleep?"

"You did?" I asked shyly. "This sounds wonderful, but I still don't understand how you could want *me*."

"How can I explain this?" He stopped to think. "Here, let me show you."

He unbuttoned the first few buttons on his shirt, exposing his bare chest. He took my hand and placed it over his heart. My palm trembled as it touched his skin. He was so perfect I gasped for a breath.

"Can you feel my heart beating?"

I nodded yes, unable to speak.

"Pay attention to the beats." He cupped my face in his hands and pressed his lips eagerly against mine, begging my mouth to open. His mouth was sweet, warm, and inviting. My head was spinning from the sensation. Unable to move, I surrendered to his touch.

"Can you feel the beating now?" he said, mingling his words with the kiss.

His heart pounded beneath by hand. I squeaked out a sound that was half a yes and half a sigh.

"That is you. I can't control the beating of my heart. You can."

I was speechless. I stared at him and tried to wrap my mind around what just happened. I must be dreaming. David was attracted to *me*. He held me against him, resting his cheek against the top of my head. I lay my head against his chest and listened to the beating beneath his skin.

Lifting my chin up to see my face, David said, "Well, my love, would you like to be my girl?"

I wasn't sure if I was dreaming or not, but if it was a dream I prayed I wouldn't wake. I nodded. He smiled back and kissed me again.

"It's getting late. I better get you home," David interrupted.

We began to walked silently back to reality. He held my hand, caressing the back of it with his thumb. We arrived at my front door too soon. I turned the key in the lock, opened the door, and prepared to step away from him. Grabbing hold of my braid, he pulled me back.

"Why do you wear you hair in a braid?

"I just want it out of the way."

"It is a pity." He brushed his hand from the top of my head down the length of my braid. "Your hair is so amazing. It has little flecks of copper and gold in it. And it feels so soft and cool against my skin. It is a shame to tie it back."

He pulled on my braid, and I tilted my head back in response. He kissed me again. "I guess it *is* better you're home now. The adjoining door would be impossible to keep shut tonight.

I blushed in reply.

We kissed again.

David whispered in my ear, "I'll see you tomorrow."

Chapter 7

Display

David made sure to see me every day. Time seemed to speed up when we were together. He would arrive at seven every evening, as was the rule in my house, and in a blink of an eye it was ten. Reluctantly, I let David go.

When we were together, it was difficult to find time to be alone. I always had a brother, sister, or both hanging around. They seemed to ignore my hints to get lost, which made me angry, but David took it all in stride. I think he actually enjoyed being near my crazy family since he had grown up without one. I was falling more love with him as I watched.

"How can you possibly put up with my family?" I asked in amazement.

"I find the whole idea of family fascinating. Don and I grew up without one. Where we come from, marriage hardly exists, let alone family. People only care about themselves, not one another. Your whole family seems so concerned for one another."

"You make it sound like you are studying us."

"In a way, I am. Where I came from, people have become corrupt. It is like they are born without souls. Maybe if people could learn to live together, like your family, there would be some hope for this world. I'd like to think some rare gene could be found that would ensure everyone would be born with a soul allowing them to glow with goodness and love… like you."

"Where do you come from? You make it sound so different from anything I've ever known. How can people be soulless?"

"It doesn't matter where I come from. I'm here now, and that is all that counts. As for being born soulless… I used to think I had no soul… until I met you."

"Everyone has a soul, and I think yours is beautiful."

He playfully bowed and said, "Well, thank you, my lady." Just then my sister ran into the room, jumped on David's back, and begged for a ride. He laughed and danced around the room with her.

David was invaluable when it came to homework. Things just made more sense when he explained it. It could be I paid closer attention to his every word than I did my teachers'.

David's best subject was history. He could describe events, times, and places as if he had personally been there. Sometimes I would feign stupidity just to have him sit close and regale me with one of his stories.

Literature involved reading, and reading was a solitary activity. David had a remedy for that. We read every novel assigned together. David read for one character and I another. Acting out the book made the story more alive and enjoyable.

It was easy to read the American novel this way, but Shakespeare's language proved more of a challenge for me.

"No matter how hard I try, I just don't understand what Shakespeare is saying. I feel like such an idiot."

"What play are you reading?

"You are going to laugh… *Romeo and Juliet*."

"You are having trouble reading *that* play?"

"I know the story, but the old English words are confusing. The way they speak is making it difficult to understand. I need to rewrite certain scenes in my own words, which is impossible if I can't fathom what they are saying."

"This play, my dear lady, contains the best pick-up lines every written." David opened the book to a particular passage and passed it to me. Pointing, he said, "We will start reading here."

Romeo had the first line, so David began speaking.

"If I profane with my unworthiest hand this holy shrine, the gentle sin is this, - My lips, two blushing pilgrims, ready stand to smooth that rough touch with a tender kiss."

He stopped and softly pressed his warm lips to the back of my hand. He looked up, and our eyes met. I couldn't breathe let alone move.

He tapped at the book. "Your turn"

"Good pilgrim, you do wrong, your hand too much, which mannerly devotion shows in this; for saints have hands that pilgrims hand do touch, and palm to palm is holy palmers' kiss."

David stood and circled behind me, then bent down to whisper in my ear.

"O, then, dear saint, let lips do what hands do; they pray, grant thou, lest faith turn to despair."

I gasped in air as I felt all the blood in my body pool in my heart. He tapped the book again.

"Saints do not move, though grant for prayers sake."

David turned me to face him.

"Then move not while my prayer's thus from my lips, by yours, my sin is purg'd."

He moved closer, and he softly kissed me. Hypnotized be his nearness, I stared into his incredible blue eyes. I knew it was Juliet's turn to speak, but how could I? I could barely breathe. I swallowed hard and tried to concentrate on reading.

"Then have my lips the sin that they have took."

He smiled and winked.

"Sin from my lips? O trespass sweetly urged, give me my sin again."

I fell into his arms for the next kiss. We kissed until one of my sisters walked in. "My homework doesn't look like that," she said.

I blushed and David returned to his side of the table, sitting down.

We were always under the watchful eyes of my family. I was afraid being on display would drive David away, but one look into his eyes and I knew he loved me too.

Chapter 8

Stranger

There were six weeks left of my senior year. Graduation and prom were just around the corner, but I didn't care. My only thoughts were about finding ways to spend the summer with Samantha… and, of course, with David.

David had moved in with Sam and Don. They gave him the entire third floor of Saltately Manor. The third floor was one huge, unfinished space. David sketched out a floor plan, dividing the space into a living room, kitchen, bath, and one bedroom. He and Don worked on the construction themselves. The work made seeing David nearly impossible. Construction filled his every free moment during the week and entirely consumed the weekends. I had to be satisfied with texting, phone calls, and stolen moments of time.

David tried to see me every night during the week, but I knew he must be exhausted, so I didn't force him to fill my daily addiction. I would call him as soon as I woke up, text him at lunch, and then he would call me after school. Our after school calls were the best. We talked the entire bus ride home, allowing us some privacy from my family's eavesdropping.

April began unusually warm, especially after winter. The spring seemed more glorious. I decided to walk around the grounds of school and enjoy the beautiful spring weather while I waited for the bus. I paced up and down, lost in thoughts of what I would write in my journal when I got home. Writing helped me miss David less.

As I walked, I looked at the houses on the street. I imaged one of them was mine. I was Mrs. David Saltate, and this was our love nest. I played out our life together in my head. Consumed by my daydreams, I had not noticed a tall, dark-haired man watching me. I thought he must be waiting for someone. There was something very compelling about him, so I observed him closer.

He was tall, thin but muscular, and appeared to be about 25 years old. He was dressed entirely in black: black jeans, black T, and a black leather jacket. His hair was straight and slightly mussed and exactly the same shade of black as his jacket. He stared back at me as if he knew me. His eyes were blue, the same exact shade of sapphire blue as David's. We continued to stare at each other as traffic passed between us, temporarily blocking our vision. When the traffic cleared, the stranger had disappeared.

My phone rang and I jumped. "Hello?"

"Hi, love, it's me. I miss you. I have been thinking about you all day. Have you been thinking of me?"

Of course I had been thinking of him, but I also felt a little guilty that I was thinking about the stranger as well. "I am always thinking of you," I said with a little guilt.

"How was school?"

"Fine. Mrs. Scott assigned *Jane Eyre* today. Do you believe it? There are only six weeks left of school, and she assigns another novel. The girls in my class nearly revolted because prom is in two weeks."

"Is that a hint for me to ask you?"

"No… I don't even want to go to prom. It is so expensive; and besides, dresses just don't hang right on me."

"I like your figure. I think you look beautiful no matter what you wear… or don't wear. You still drive me crazy."

"Will I see you tonight?"

"I wish I could, but Don and I are going to work on the plumbing tonight. Believe me, I would much rather be with you. I feel badly enough about neglecting you. I hope you don't find someone else."

"I told you before, David, you are the *only* one who wants me, and I don't even know why you do."

"If the world can't see how special you are, so be it. But if they ever notice you, God help me, I hope I can compete."

"You, Mr. Saltate, have nothing to worry about. I want you so much it is all I can think about."

"So… are we going to the prom together?"

"I would have to go shopping for a dress."

"I would be honored to take you."

"What fun would it be for you to watch me dress and undress until I found something that fit?"

"I don't know about the dress part, but the undress sounds fun."

"David, you are terrible. I have to go. I see my bus coming. I love you."

"I love you too."

I hung up my phone and placed it in my bag, boarded the bus, and found a seat. I settled in to the ride, looking out the window. I watched passengers board on and off at each stop. Then my heart skipped a beat. The stranger entered and sat one seat in front of me on the opposite side.

He was alone. I tried to tell myself there was nothing to worry about. He was just traveling in the same direction I was. He probably didn't even know I existed. Besides, why should I care if he noticed me? I tried to swallow and pretend like I didn't notice him.

Just then my phone rang, startling me. I answered the phone but said nothing.

I recognized my mom's voice. "Hello, Ally?"

"Yes, Mom."

"I'm all out of bread and milk, and I need them for dinner. Can you stop by the market on your way home and pick them up for me?"

"Sure. I'm on the bus now. I'll stop at the market and should be home soon. Is there anything else you needed?"

"Maybe some cookies for dessert."

"Cookies. Got it. I'll see you soon."

I put my phone back in my bag and looked up at the stranger. He was looking out the window with his back to me. I decided I was making this more dramatic than it was, so I returned to looking out my window. When my stop arrived, I walked past the stranger and out the front door of the bus, leaving him behind.

I walked into the market then up and down the aisles, picking up the various items as instructed. I checked to make sure I had enough money and headed to the register. As I walked, I saw a flash of black blur by the corner of my eye. When I reached the end of the aisle, I casually looked around. It was then I saw the stranger staring back at me. He *was* following me. I hadn't exaggerated this in my head.

In a panic, I grabbed my cell phone and called David.

"Miss me already?" David answered.

"David, I think there is a man following me."

"Where are you?"

"I stopped by the market on my way home to pick up a few things for my mother. Oh, David, I saw him at school, then on the bus, and now he is here. What should I do?"

"Stay there. I'm coming. You'll be safe as long as you stay in the market. Don't go anywhere near him and don't leave the market."

"I won't. Please hurry. I'm scared."

"I closer than you think. I was driving to surprise you when you called. I'm about twenty minutes away. I'll be there soon."

"I can wait. Just don't hang up on me."

"I won't. I couldn't. What does he look like?"

"He is tall, all dressed in black, with black hair and blue eyes. I think he is about your age, maybe a little older."

I looked back down the aisle, but I didn't see the stranger. His absence didn't bring me any solace. I was still frightened. I needed David.

I walked up and down the aisles of the store pretending to be searching for something to purchase, but all along I was really looking for the stranger. David kept talking to me.

"Is he anywhere near you?"

"No, I don't see him now, but I'm still afraid."

"I'm almost to the parking lot. Where are you in the store?"

"I'm walking up and down the aisles. I'm too afraid to stand still."

"Meet me by the entrance. You'll be…"

My phone cut off. I looked down, no bars. I walked quickly to the entrance. I kept telling myself I would be fine. The stranger was nowhere in sight, and I would be in David's arms soon. I wasn't watching were I was going, and I turned a corner too quickly and bumped right into the stranger. He caught me in his arms to stop my fall. His arms held me firm. I was too afraid to make eye contact with him, so I stared straight into his chest. "Are you okay?" he said.

I wiggled back and forth to break his grip on my arms, but he held me firm. It was then I noticed a pendent hanging from his neck exactly like the one David always wore. How was it possible for them both to be wearing the same pendent? My struggling finally broke me free, and I turned to run. I saw David entering the market and rushed to him. He wrapped his arms tightly around me, pulling me close. I breathed a sigh of relief and hugged my protector tightly.

David looked over my head at the stranger still watching us. He kissed my forehead and said, "Wait here."

"No, David, don't leave me. I'm afraid."

"You'll be fine. I just want to talk to him."

"No." But David left and walked to confront the stranger.

"Are you out of your mind? If you have some vendetta with me, here I am. Leave her out of this!"

"I was just observing her. She *is* a very powerful Halo." The stranger spoke to David as if they knew one another.

"Keep *that* to yourself, please," David answered, pushing the stranger back.

Undeterred, the stranger responded, "I guess you didn't tell her why you are here?"

"I'll tell her in my own time. Now leave her alone."

"I'll leave, but you know I'll be back. You and I have unfinished business." The stranger pushed past David, bowed in my direction, and then walked out of the market.

David returned to me, and I was once more in the safety of his arms.

"Do you know him?" I asked.

"No."

"But it sounded like you knew him. I heard you talking."

"He won't bother you again. You are safe."

"David, tell me the truth. You know him, don't you?"

"Why would you think that?"

"I saw you. You recognized one another. Besides, he has a pendent just like yours. What are you not telling me?"

David hurried me out of the market, ignoring my questions. When we were in his car, he turned and said, "Alright, I do know him."

"Who is he? What does he want? Why was he following me?"

"He wants me. He thinks the easiest way to get to me is through you, but you're safe now. I'll take care of everything. You don't have to worry about him anymore."

"David, please tell me what is going on. Who is he?"

"Not here, not now. I'll drop you off at home. I'll call you tonight."

"Please just tell me who he is and what does he want with you?"

"His name is Tom. He is my half-brother, and what he wants is too complex to get into now. I promise, I'll tell you everything. Now go. I'll call you tonight."

David kissed me and drove off, leaving me standing in front of my house, full of questions.

Chapter 9

Alone

I impatiently waited for David's call, but when he did our conversation was strained. He sidestepped every question I asked with banter. If I asked him a direct question, he cut the call short with some lame excuse. David also couldn't seem to find time to see me. He politely would break our dates using reasons like work or illness. It didn't take long for me to figure out David was getting rid of me.

Filled with concern, I called Samantha to see if she knew anything.

"Hi, Sam, it's me, Ally Kat. How have you been?"

"I'm getting pretty lonely at Saltately Manor. I'm almost desperate enough to look for a job. How are things with you?"

"How can you be lonely? Isn't Don with you?"

"He seems to be spending most of his time with David. When they are not working on the third-floor apartment, they are running off together to take care of some business. When I try to talk to Don, I get useless conversation in return. It is like David and he have a secret they are keeping. Don't get me wrong. I like David. He is a great brother, but I want my husband back."

I knew exactly how she felt. David and Don were keeping something from us. I continued to pry for information. Maybe Sam had seen the stranger.

"Is there anyone else hanging out at the Manor? I mean helping with them with the attic apartment?"

"No, it is always just the two of them. I told Don to hire someone, but they insist on doing the work alone. I think it is an excuse to allow them more time to work on the secret they share."

"David has been acting stranger lately too. His behavior is beginning to worry me."

"I wouldn't worry. I think they are both just tired, and we are making too much out of this. I think David wants the apartment finished as soon as possible. I'm sure that is all it is. Don would never keep secrets from me."

Maybe she could rationalize away her feelings, but I couldn't. It was clear Sam didn't know anything about the stranger. I would have to go to David if I wanted any answers, but how could I get him to talk?

David's calls dwindled to once a week. He never came to see me. I knew it marked the end. All the life had been sucked out of me and only a void was left to take its place. I cried until there were no more tears left in me. I was numb.

Time carried on in David's absence. One day was just like the day before, indiscernible.

My phone rang, and I jumped. I looked down to see who was calling. It read DAVID. I took a deep breath and answered.

"Hello?" I said, full of fear. This was it, the moment I was dreading, the moment that drained sleep from me, the moment when David would finally tell me good-bye.

"Can you get out tonight?" he asked.

He wanted to see me as he destroyed me. I couldn't face him.

"Can't you just say what you need to say over the phone?"

"No. It's been an eternity since I saw you, and what I need to do can only be done in person. Can you be free by seven? I can meet you in front of your house."

I reluctantly said yes, but he hung up before I could say anything else.

I waited in front of my house that evening thinking I was glutton for punishment. If this was the end, I had to see him one last time no matter how much it killed me.

He pulled up and leaned across the seat, opening the passenger door of his convertible. I took a deep breath and stepped in. He reached for me with his hand and turned my face and kissed me quickly.

"What is wrong?" He asked, noticing my unresponsive lips.

"David, I wish you would just get it over with. It's killing me."

"Get what over with?"

"Breaking up. Go ahead and tell me you are through with me."

"God, no, what would make you think I want to break up?"

"You haven't seen me for weeks. You hardly call. It is okay. I knew this day would come. I knew you'd wake up and see you could do so much better than me."

"I'm so sorry. I didn't realize how much I have been neglecting you. Please forgive me. I hope to make it up to you tonight."

"Where are we going?" I asked as he pulled away from the front of my house.

"I want to show you what I've been working on."

That was all he said. He offered no reason for his absence these past few weeks. I thought about starting the dreaded subject up again but decided against it. My question would wait. I was glad just to be near him.

We drove to Saltately Manor. David parked, and we walked to the front door. The house looked strange, dark and abandoned. Not a single light radiated, and silence engulfed us.

"Where are Sam and Don?" I asked.

"They are out for the evening. Don surprised Sam with concert tickets and booked a hotel room for the night." He took my hand and led me through the dark entryway into the living room.

"Then we are alone?" I asked.

"Completely," he answered while starting a fire in the fireplace. The embers gave the room a soft golden glow. David did not turn on any of the lights. He pulled throw pillows from the chairs, tossing them onto the floor in front of the fireplace. Kneeling in the center of his makeshift bed, he extended his hand up to me, inviting me to join him.

I had never been alone with David before. I wondered what he expected. I hesitated for a moment and then took his hand. I knew I could not deny David anything.

David must have read my thoughts. "I know we have never really been alone before, but you can trust me." He reached for my face, caressing my cheek and neck. "I've missed you so much. It seems like forever."

I could barely swallow let alone breathe. All rational thought left me. David's eyes held me in a trance.

"I want you to relax. You are safe with me. All I want is a real kiss."

Relax. Sure, that was easy for him to say. I'm sure his blood didn't rush with anticipation. I wondered if he could hear my heart pounding.

He lightly ran his finger across my bottom lip, opening my mouth ever so slightly. "The soft inner part of your lips has more feeling," he said, letting his finger linger. His eyes ran up and down my body, taking me in.

I didn't care what happened next. I put my arms around his neck, weaving my fingers into the curls of his blond hair. My lips reached for his. We kissed with a passion so deep it felt like our souls fused together. We continued to kiss softly and gently in the darkness of the room.

David stopped only to take off his shirt. The amber light from the fire tanned his skin, accentuating every muscular curve. The black crystal necklace he wore glimmered in the moonlight streaming in from the window. He laid me down on the stone of the hearth. The stone was cold on my back in contrast to the warmth of his skin against mine.

I leaned forward and kissed his chest. I could feel his heart pounding as he breathed deeply.

He pulled on my braid, and I lifted my head back to meet his. "You trust me, don't you?" he said, mingling his words with a kiss.

"Yes," I whispered.

"Then don't stop me." He unbuttoned the front of my blouse. He kissed me deeply, feeling my skin with his hands. He stopped caressing me for just a moment, taking off the pendent he wore and placing it around my neck. He ran his fingers down the silver chain and brushed the contours of my breasts, retrieving the stone. He cradled me in his arms and rolled me onto the soft pile of pillows. The satin felt deliciously cool against my bare back. He pressed down on me and then—

The lights burst on, intruding in our interlude.

"What are you doing?" Don's voice shattered the silence and the moment. Embarrassed, I tried to grope for my shirt, but the weight of David's body inhibited my movement.

"Are you out of your mind? What were you going to do? Did you even tell her what would happen if you leapt with only one stone? For God's sake, Dave, she's just a kid."

I squirmed to free myself from under David. Once I was free, I stood holding David's shirt in front of me.

David stood, shielding me from Don, and confronted him. "Will you please be quiet and let me handle this? What are you doing home anyway?"

"Sam wasn't feeling well, so I brought her home. Thank God she went up the back stairs and didn't walk in on this."

Don turned his attention to me. "I can't believe you were willing to go along with this crazy idea."

David pushed Don back, shielding me.

Don returned David's glare, saying, "You didn't tell her, did you?"

"I was going to tell her, but something stopped me," David replied.

Tears began to stream down my face. I gasped for each breath, choking out, "I want to go home."

David and Don turned their attention to me. Just the looks on their faces accelerated my cries to the point of screaming. David reached for me to offer some comfort, but I pulled away and repeated my request to be taken home.

"I'll take you home as soon as you calm down."

"I want to go home now!" I screamed and started to pound my hands against his chest.

"Alright, alright…I'll take you home." David handed me my blouse and pushed Don out of the living room and into the hall. Coldly he said to his brother, "I'll deal with you when I come back."

I quickly buttoned my blouse and raced to the front door, still crying. David tried to put his arm around me, but I couldn't let him touch me. He opened the front door, and I ran to the car. He gently put his hand on my back while he unlocked the passenger door for me, but his touch sent me into hysterics. I clung to the passenger door, continuing my sobs.

"Please try to calm down. Try not to listen to that stuff Don said. Don't let him upset you." David brushed the back of my head with his hand, but I recoiled from his touch. "You know I would never hurt you, don't you?"

I exploded. "Hurt me? That's all you do is hurt me. Ever since the incident with the stranger, you won't answer my questions. You avoid me like the plague and then drag me to a deserted house. You were the one who seduced me into making love. You know I can't think straight when it comes to you, and you took advantage of it."

David said nothing in response. He sat silently for the rest of the ride, listening to me cry. When we reached my house, I opened the door, running from the car before he could stop me. I disappeared into my house, locking the door behind me. I didn't want to take the chance that David would follow.

Chapter 10

Answers

David called me continually for the next two weeks, but I instructed my family to tell him I didn't wish to talk to him and hang up. Just the sound of his voice forced me to remember how he had planned to take advantage of me. I was left confused and destroyed, raw. It was as if I received shock therapy to cure my insanity. I had been living in a dream world, and the arrival of reality had shattered the orb I existed in. I had to put David out of my mind and heart if I was to survive. I knew only time and distance would be my salvation.

David had left me shattered and full of unanswered questions. Events from our time together played repeatedly in my mind, driving me closer to the edge of insanity.

I always settled on one event as the catalyst of change in our relationship: the stranger's arrival. Why did the stranger follow me that day? David certainly knew him. He actually said the stranger was his half-brother who was looking for him, a brother Sam and I knew nothing about. The strangers had said he was "observing me" and I was a "powerful Halo." Halo was a word David once used when referring to me. What did it mean?

Then there was everything Don said the night he walked in on us. Don said it was foolish, almost dangerous, to leap two people with one stone. Leap… leap where? My mind rocked back and forth in an effort to make sense of everything.

Even though I had no contact with David, I pictured him everywhere: the halls of school, walking down the street, in the shadows of the night, everywhere.

David, however, kept his distance. The daily calls subsided. It was apparent he was moving on also. Time and distance were erasing me from his memory.

The pieces of my heart ached with every thought. I prayed God would help me understand why He allowed David to come into my life only to have him leave.

I walked slowly home from church one Sunday as if in a trance. Everything about the early summer morning reminded me of David: the breeze softly caressing my skin the way he did, the golden flowers in the same shade as his hair, and the crystal blue sky the same shade as his eyes. Dear God, will I ever have him out of my system?

I was stopped by another apparition of David's body crested against the trunk of a tree. He stood motionless in my vision dressed in the same blue shirt he wore that night. Blue made his eyes even more compelling. *I must be severely heartbroken or have completely lost my mind to induce such a vivid hallucination*, I thought.

I continued walking toward the vision, and then it spoke.

I blinked, but the vision remained. He stepped from the shadows of the tree, and I realized David was truly standing in front of me.

"You have to let me talk to you. Please."

He waited for me to respond, but I said nothing.

"Ally, please, you have to let me explain."

I had tried so diligently to avoid this moment. I knew if I saw David again I would lose my resolve. Trying to stay strong, I looked away and said, "I'm not supposed to see you or talk to you any more."

"Please, just a few minutes. Let me at least walk you home."

"You can't. My parents have forbidden me from making any contact with you," I said as I pushed my way past him.

"For God's sake, Allyson, look at me," he pleaded. "I can't eat or sleep. I'm going out of my mind without you."

I stopped and looked at David. His beautiful blue eyes were tired and bloodshot like those of some hopeless creature. I could feel the pain reflected in his face. Moved, I touched his cheek with my hand. He leaned his head into my palm in an effort to hold me to him.

"You can walk me home, but we have to walk down another street. We can't run into my father." I took David's hand and lead the way.

David held my hand, caressing the back of it with his thumb. His hold was soft, but the firmness convinced me he had no intention of letting me go.

"What did you tell you parents? I mean, about what happened?" David asked.

"I told them you took me to Sam's place, but they weren't home. We were kissing, you got carried away and tried to force yourself on me." I could see the hurt my explanation inflicted on him.

"You know I would never hurt you or use you like that."

"Well, what was I supposed to tell them? You fill me with questions, seduce me, and leave me devastated."

"No, I suppose I did make a mess of things."

"Yes, you did. All I want to know is why. Why did you shut me out? What is it you're not telling me? I know you are hiding something. I can feel it. I can't take it anymore, David. Do you have any idea what you do to me, or don't you care?"

"I care. I suppose it started out just as a game, but I had no idea how powerful you are. You stole my heart and all rational thought with it. I was content to stay here with you, forever, but then Tom showed up. I couldn't let him take you. I had to do something."

"Take me where? You still haven't told me who Tom is or what he wants with me."

"There is so much to tell you. I was afraid if I told you everything, you may not want to see me any more. I was an idiot. I know now telling you is the only thing I can do. Can you ever forgive me?"

"Do you promise to answer *all* my questions?"

"Yes… Can I please hold you before I fall completely to pieces?"

I wrapped by arms around David's waist and pressed by head against his chest. I could feel his heart pounding. He ran his hands down each of my arms, outlining my body until he reached my waist, then he lifted me off my feet until we were face to face. His arms slid around me, locking us together, and we kissed. His kiss was warm, exciting, passionate, and familiar. If I had any doubts of how David felt, this kiss erased them.

"Thank God I have you back again," he whispered into my ear.

"I don't know what good it will do. My parents have decided I'm not to see you anymore."

"There must be a way you can get out. I have so much to tell you, but it can't be done here."

He looked at me fearfully. How bad was the secret he kept? I knew I had to find a way for us to be together. "Where is your car?" I asked.

"I parked it a few blocks away and walked. I was afraid you would avoid me if you saw my car. Why?"

"Go get your car and meet me back here. I'm going home. I'll make up some kind of an excuse, tell them a lie, give them a reason, I don't know. I'll get out some way and meet you here." He nodded, and I slipped myself from under his arm.

I turned to run home, but David grabbed me and pulled be back. He kissed me one more time and let me go. I jolted for home, turning only once to make sure he still was watching me.

My mind raced trying to think of some reason to leave again once I arrived home.

"Your face is flushed," noticed my mother.

I covered with a lie. "I ran all the way from the church."

"You're late. Church was over almost an hour ago."

"I ran into Victoria, and we got to talking. We are working on a project together for school. She said the paper we saved on her computer was lost when her system crashed. She asked if I could go back to school to work on the paper with her."

I didn't wait for permission. I quickly threw a few school items into my backpack just to make my lie more real and headed for the door.

"I don't know when I will be home. I have my cell, so I will check in."

"You are going to school on a Sunday?"

"No. Did I say school? I meant the library." Another lie, but I didn't care. I just wanted to get back to David.

I grabbed my jacket, kissed my mother, and flew down the stairs and out the door. I ran the block back to where David was waiting. He reached across the seat, opening the door, and I jumped in.

"Where are we going?" I asked.

"You'll see when we get there. If I'm going to tell you everything, it can only be at one particular place, and it is about an hour's drive away."

I nestled myself against the side of David's body as he drove silently. I could tell he was worried about my reaction to what he was about to tell me. His silence worried me. Maybe this was the end of us. It was a feeling I couldn't shake. I knew I couldn't live without him, but I was sure he could live without me.

We finally pulled off the highway and onto a dirt road. The road twisted and wound through a grove of trees. The desolate landscape was void of any human contact. Why did he need such an isolated spot to talk to me? Worried, I wrapped my arms tightly around his right arm and clung to his body. I'm sure he could feel my trepidation, but he offered no support. He just stared unresponsively at the winding dirt road ahead of us.

David pulled off the dirt road, driving on the prairie grass, and then stopped the car. He looked down at me with concern in his eyes.

"We're here," is all he said. He got out of the car and held his hand back to me. I unbuckled my seatbelt, reaching for him in response. He gently pulled me to my feet and then let go. He turned and paced away from me into the field.

"Where are we?" I called after him.

He stopped and turned to look at me.

"This is it, my home. This is where I live... or where I *will* live."

Confused, I shook my head.

"In the time I came from, *this* is where my home is. Of course, nothing is here now, but in the future this is where I will live and grow up." He wanted for me to respond. "I'm sure this is a lot for you to take in. I want to tell you everything. No more secrets. Maybe it would be easier if you asked me questions."

"What are you trying to tell me? You are from the future?"

He nodded. "I'm a time traveler."

"What time are you from?"

"I was born in the year 2225."

"Okay... How old are you, then?"

"I can't measure time like you do. Time stops and starts when I leap, so it is impossible to measure. I have used IDs claiming my age any where from seventeen to about twenty-seven. The ID I have right now says I'm twenty-one."

"So you are about five years older than me?" I said, dazed.

"Actually *you* are about two hundred years older than me if we go by birth records."

He smiled in hopes of giving me some reassurance but confusion still engulfed me. He took a deep breath, walked to me, and took my hands in his. He put his head down to touch our foreheads together and waited.

Trying to make some sense of what I was hearing, I asked, "Why did you come here?"

He lifted my face with his hands, staring down at me with his piecing blue eyes, and said, slowly, "I came here for you."

I knew I had to keep asking questions. I wanted to understand, but everything seemed so surreal.

"Is David Saltate your real name?"

"I was born David 4249. In my time, it is easier to separate people by numbers instead of last names. Most children are produced in test tubes, like Don and I. Numbers make it easy to identify which donors you come from. When Don and I started our time traveling, it was necessary to have last names, so we decided on Saltate, based on the crystal that allows us to time travel."

"So your pendent is how you… leap. It's made of saltate not onyx?"

"Actually it is made of saltanium. Saltanium is a blend of man-made atoms. These atoms contain properties that can open a worm hole, facilitating time travel."

"How do you… time travel?"

"I have to hold the crystal in my hand, close to my chest, and squeeze it while thinking of a time and destination, and I'm… there."

"What does it feel like to leap?"

"It doesn't hurt. It is like falling asleep and waking up in a different time."

"You said you came here for me. Why?"

David took a deep breath and exhaled slowly. He looked concerned, as if the answer my question may not be something I want to know.

"This is complicated, so let me start from the beginning. Don is researching the origin of a mutated gene. Saltanium aids him in his search. I have always accompanied Don on his leaps and helped him with his research. We requested permission to leap this time, but at the last minute, my request was denied. I leapt anyway, breaking the law, and now I am wanted for being a spore."

"A spore?" I repeated.

"A spore is someone running through time without permission. The governing body of my time has sent a falcon to bring me back."

"Then you are leaving me?"

"I could never leave you. I tried to take you with me…"

"You were going to leap with me that night, but Don walked in and stopped you."

"My crystal can only safely carry one person. That is why I put it on you. I also thought skin-to-skin contact would make the leap safer for you. I was planning on leaping with you and explaining everything to you later. I thought I had it under control, but I forgot one very important thing."

"What?"

"The feeling of your body next to mine… Let's just say you affect my concentration. All I could think about was how much I wanted you."

I blushed and hid by face against his chest. "I wanted you too," I whispered.

He pulled on my braid, and I responded by lifting my lips to his. I felt safe and comfortable in his arms. I did not care who, what, where, or when he was, as long as he was mine.

"Do you have any other questions?"

"Just one. Who was the stranger, and why was he following me?"

"The stranger's name is Tom. I guess you could say he is my half-brother. Tom, Don, and I have the same donor mother, but our family bonds end there. Tom is a falcon, a policeman, and he has a job to do. I don't think anything can stop him. I've been leaping back and forth through time these past weeks in hopes of losing him. I think it may have worked, but I don't know for how long. Besides, I could never leave you. You are my life now."

"It still doesn't explain why he was following me. Why not just follow you?"

"It is true that Tom will be paid a bounty for returning me, but while looking for me, he found something even more valuable."

"Don?"

"No…you."

"Me! Why would he want me?"

"You, my love, are the origin of the Halo gene. Don's research traced the gene back to Samantha, but after testing her DNA, she proved not to be the source. Do you remember the day you hurt your hand?"

I nodded yes.

"Don took some blood samples from you and tested them. The results show *you* are the source. Tom must have found and read Don's report, so he switched his tracking from me to you. I've lost him in time for now, but I know he will not give up. That is why I can't let you out of my sight. I need to protect you all day and all night."

"I'm sure my parents will never let you spend all day and all night with me."

"What if I told you there was a way for us to be together—live together, sleep together—and no one would care or object?"

"That's impossible."

"No, it isn't." He looked at me earnestly. "I want you to think about what I'm going to say. I thought about it, and I know it's the only answer."

"What? You are scaring me."

"There is nothing to be afraid of." He knelt down in front of me, looked up at me, and slowly said, "Will you marry me?"

"Marry you?" I couldn't believe what I was hearing. "Are you sure?"

"I'm sure. I just want you to be."

"Are you doing this because you *have to*… to protect me?"

"I'm doing this because I *love* you and *want* to protect you."

"My parents are not going to allow me to get married. I'm barely seventeen and still in school."

"I thought about that too. So we are going to elope."

"Elope?"

"All you have to do is say yes. Please say yes."

"You *really* want to marry me?"

"Yes, without hesitation or doubt. I love you."

"This is crazy."

"Then let's be crazy."

I looked in his eyes and said, "Yes, I'll marry you."

He stood up smiling. His eyes sparkled as he said, "May I please hold you before I go completely mad?"

I hung my arms around his neck, pulling him to me. We kissed passionately.

David's lips moved from mine, making a soft trail of kisses until he reached my ear, then he whispered, "We better get going. Sam is waiting."

He kissed my shocked face on the forehead and pulled me back to the car.

Chapter 11

Together

"What do you mean, Sam is waiting for us?" He had just asked me to marry him, and now he was racing to some destination. I was excited and confused.

"I told Sam I was going to ask you to marry me, and, well, you know Sam. She just got carried away with all the planning."

"What planning?" I asked, almost afraid to know the answer.

He took his eyes off the road for just a second to look at me. Smiling he said, "Our wedding."

"Wait, Sam is planning our wedding... today?"

"She is so excited about it. It's all she has done for the last two days."

"How did she know I would say yes?"

"How could you refuse me?" he teased with an impish grin.

I sat quietly. My mind raced as David sped us along to our wedding. Everything was happening so fast my head was spinning.

We pulled up in front of Sam and Don's house, and Sam came running out to greet us. Excitedly, she opened the car door and pulled me from my seat.

"We have to hurry. I didn't think it would take Dave so long to convince you. I knew I wanted to marry Don before he could finish asking the question," she joked. Sam continued pulling me toward the front door and into the house.

The house was bathed in the scent of roses. Huge bouquets of pink roses filled every inch of the living room. I tried to stop and enjoy the beauty, but Sam barked out, "I'll take Ally upstairs so we can get ready. Don, you take David into the study so he can change. The minister will be here any minute. We have to hurry."

Sam whisked me upstairs and pushed me into the bedroom I once occupied. There were some clothes laid out on the bed, and she began to pull at my clothes, trying to get them off.

"We have to hurry and get dressed. I still have to do your hair and make-up. Here," she said, handing me a two-piece beige suit. "Put this on while I get dressed."

I slipped off my jeans and shirt and put on the suit as directed. It was a beautiful shade of cream-colored linen with bright white piping around the collar. I stepped into a pair of white heels and turned to look at Samantha.

She looked radiant. She wore a beautiful blue floral-print dress. Being taller, her dress hung perfectly, accenting every curve of her body.

"It isn't fair. The bride is supposed to be the one everyone is looking at and you look amazing."

"We are not finished with you yet. Besides, I think David only has eyes for you."

Sam began to work on my hair. I sat on the edge of the bed while she undid my braid and brushed my hair. It was at that moment I awoke from my dream-like state.

"Oh my God, I told my mother I was going to the library. She will expect me home for dinner. What time is it?"

"Relax. I called and told them I ran into you, and you will be staying overnight with me. In the morning, I'll drive over and break the news to them about your elopement."

"They are going to kill you first and then me."

"I'll take care of everything. It is the least a maid-of-honor can do. Besides, I kind of blindsided them when I eloped, so I'm an old hand at smoothing things over. There, your hair is done. Now let's take care of the traditions and get this wedding started."

"But my hair is just combed."

"David left particular instructions: No braid."

Just then, there was a knock on the bedroom door. Sam answered it, talking to the closed door. "Who is it?"

"It's David. The flowers arrived."

"Just leave them by the door, and I'll take care of them."

"Can't I give them to Ally myself?"

Sam opened the door a crack and said, "You are not jinxing this wedding by seeing the bride before the ceremony."

"Please let me just hand her the flowers and talk to her for a minute."

"Very well. You can talk to her through the door; but remember, no peeking!"

Sam waved to me, and I walked to the door. David's arm appeared through the crack Sam guarded holding an amazing bouquet. The bouquet was composed of every flower imaginable.

"Oh, David, they're lovely," I said, taking the bouquet from him.

"I didn't know what color dress Sam picked out for you, so I told the florist to give me one of everything."

"The flowers are just perfect. I've never seen a bouquet like this. Thank you."

"Okay, that is enough," Sam ordered. She pushed David's hand out and shut the door. "Let's get this wedding started. As your maid-of-honor, it is my job to make sure you have something old. I found this pin in an antique store, and I thought it would be perfect for you."

Samantha handed me a small box, and I opened it. Inside was a pin in the shape of an anchor. It was made of gold and enhanced with inlaid pieces of red glass. She took the pin from my hand and pinned it to the jacket of the suit.

"I liked the anchor," she said. It is the symbol of hope and strength. Remember to always be each other's anchor and to give each other hope. Well, that takes care of your something old. Your something new are the flowers Dave gave you, and your something borrowed is my suit you're wearing. I think that takes care of everything, so shall we go?"

"Wait, I need something blue."

"You'll get that downstairs." She smiled, open the door, and we walked to the top or the staircase.

I stood there with Samantha one step below me. She signaled to Don, and the sound of classical music filled the house. The music seemed to come from all around us. Small bouquets of pink roses, dotted by yards of lace, wound down the railings leading us into the living room. Larger baskets of pink and red roses formed and aisle ending at the fireplace. White candles of every size illuminated the room, and the light of the sunset made golden panels of the windows. A minister waited in front of the fireplace with Don and David at his left.

Samantha turned to me and said, "Here we go."

For a second, I was frozen in fear. Was this the right thing to do? Everything had happened so fast.

Sam pulled at me, and we descended the stairs to the living room. Whatever doubts I had vanished as soon as I saw David. He was dressed entirely in blue: blue suit, blue shirt, and blue silk tie. The only thing he wore that was not blue was a single pure white rose on his lapel.

I looked into his amazing blue eyes and said, "I guess you are my something blue."

"You said blue was your favorite color."

David took my hand, and we looked at the minister.

The minister began, "Dearly beloved, we are gathered here today to join this man and this woman in the bond of holy matrimony. If anyone can show just cause why these two people should not be joined, let them speak now or ever after hold their peace. "Do you, David, take this woman to be your wedded wife?"

"I do."

"David, you may say your vows now."

David turned to me, looking down with his amazing blue eyes, and said, "I, David, take you, Allyson, to be my wife. I promise to love you, protect you, and stand by you through all time."

"Do you, Allyson, take this man to be your wedded husband?"

I knew it was my turn to speak, but for a moment I panicked. I had no vows prepared. I looked at David and knew in an instant what I wanted to say to him.

"I, Allyson Katherine Baker, take you, David, to be my husband. I thank God for bringing you into my life. Knowing you has changed me beyond all my imaginings. I will love you, honor you, and cherish you all the days of my life until the end of time."

The minister then signaled for the ring. David reached into the breast pocket of his suit, pulling out a white gold band anchored by a marquise-cut black onyx stone. Two small diamonds guarded each side of the stone. The minister blessed the ring and said, "Please place the ring on Allyson's finger and repeat after me—"

David interrupted saying, "With this ring, I thee wed. Please wear it as a sign of our love for each other." He then slid the ring onto my finger.

"I now pronounce you husband and wife. You may kiss." David wrapped his arms around my waist and lifted me up until we were face to face. We kissed to seal our promise to each other.

After the ceremony, Samantha hurried us into the dining room. The only light provided was from a dozen of candles flickering romantically around the room. The table was set for four. Each place was graced with her finest china, silver, and crystal. A small, elegant, three-tier wedding cake stood as the centerpiece. Real pink roses danced up the sides of the cake to a crystal heart cresting on the top. The heart reflected back every flicker of the candlelight, dancing sparkles around the room as if it were alive.

We feasted on soup, salad, steamed vegetables, wild rice, and lobster. The four of us ate, drank, and laughed comfortably.

After dinner, Don stood up, opened a magnum of champagne, and poured everyone a glass.

"It is my pleasure, as best man, to toast my little brother and my new sister. Thank you, Ally, for taking David off my hands. I wish you all the best in anchoring him in one place." He raised his glass in a toast.

I quickly responded, "Did you forget I'm the only one here who isn't twenty-one yet?"

"It is all right, Mrs. Saltate, you can sip from mine," David said as he pulled my chair closer to him.

Sam stood up. "I'd like to make a toast, as maid-of-honor. To my little sister, Ally, I hope you and David are as happy as Don and I."

After sharing a sip with David, I took the glass and stood.

"I —we would like to toast Samantha and Don for making this the most perfect wedding anyone could ever imagine. It is all so unbelievable. I feel like a princess in a fairy tale. Thank you."

After our toast, Samantha announced, "Well, it is getting late. It is high time you two were off to bed. We have to get this honeymoon started."

I had not thought about *that* part of being married. It was true I loved David, but I had never... What if I didn't know what to do? I was unable to move when David gently took my hand and slowly pulled me from the room.

At the base of the second staircase, just off the kitchen and leading to the third floor of the house, David lifted me into his arms. "Well, Mrs. Saltate, shall we see our new home?" Resting my head against David's shoulder, he swiftly climbed the stairs.

A massive oak door waited at the top. David instructed me to open it since I still occupied both his arms. I reached down from my perch and turned the knob. The door silently swung open.

"I can't wait to show you around. I hope you like it." David placed me on my feet and turned on the lights. "This is entrance hall. I put a closet on one length of the wall for extra storage."

I nodded in recognition.

He turned a corner, leading us into the next room. It was a large open space, really almost three rooms in one. A large, masculine, black leather couch stood in the middle of the space. It was flanked on each side by matching black leather armchairs. The couch faced a small gas fireplace with a plasma TV hanging above. Solid, bright red European pillows were casually placed on the couch. Large, black, sculpted iron lamps flanked tables on either side of the couch, providing the only light. A large white shag rug covered the wood floor in front of the fireplace.

David then pulled me to the galley-style kitchen. One wall was covered with maple cabinets. The top cabinets had glass-windowed doors, and I could see bold red dishes filling the shelves. A black refrigerator stood on one side of the black granite counters, and a black stove balanced it on the other. A separate space in the far corner held a table and chairs.

David pulled me to the far end of the great room, opening another door. "This is our bedroom."

I followed him into the room. This room was in sharp contrast to the rest of the apartment. It was soft and feminine. A large, four-poster bed stood against the far wall. A white quilt with small, embroidered, blue forget-me-nots dotted between ribbons and lace covered the bed. Small crystal lamps rested on nightstands.

David pulled me further into the room and opened the door to bathroom. Pure white marble ran across the floor and up the walls. A large two-sink vanity with matching mirrors stood opposite the door. Royal blue bath sheets hung from a golden bar, and soft blue towels hung on top. The bathtub looked more like a private pool. A skylight above the tub opened to night sky.

I didn't notice David moving closer to me. The sound of his voice whispering in my ear shot electricity through me.

"I'll let you use the bathroom first while I get ready for bed."

I nodded and closed the door. Filled with apprehension, I undressed and got into the shower. I was a little afraid about what would happen next. I didn't know if I was ready to be a wife. I also didn't want to disappoint David. I stood in the shower until the water ran cold. I turned off the water, pulled back the curtain, and reached for a towel, but all the towels were missing. I looked for my clothes, but they were gone also. I was not prepared to leave the bathroom naked, so I pulled the shower curtain closed, hiding myself, and called for David.

"David, can you bring me a towel?"

"I have one right here." His voice startled me. He was on the other side of the shower curtain. I began to tremble. I peaked around the curtain and saw David standing with the bath sheet opened, waiting for me.

"Please… just hand me the towel. I'm too embarrassed to come out."

"You have to come out eventually. I'll wait."

"David," I said reluctantly. "This is really embarrassing."

"Come to me."

I decided the best way to handle my dilemma was to just do it. I closed my eyes, flung open the shower curtain, and stepped from the tub. David wrapped the towel around me and lifted me into his arms.

"Believe me, lady, you have nothing to be embarrassed about."

I rested my head against his shoulder and let him carry me to the bed. He laid me down and then lay down next to me. He put his arm around me and began to gently kiss my neck. My heart was pounding out of my chest. He must have been able to feel me shaking. He stopped kissing me.

Softly caressing my face, he said, "We don't have to do anything if you don't want to."

"I want to… it is just… that…I've never done this before. Have you?"

"Let's just say I'm not new to the process, but it's okay to be a little afraid. I'm scared too. You see, I've never been in love before, so this is new to me too."

He ran his fingers through my long damp hair. I looked into his loving eyes and took a deep breath, letting out a relaxing sigh.

He rested the side of his face against mine, whispering, "I love you." He kissed my ear, my neck, my chin, moving until his lips brushed against mine. He rested his body on mine and continued to kiss me until the towel between us disappeared.

Chapter 12
Morning

I rolled between consciousness and dreams like a tide moving to and from a shore. The house was still void of any sound or movement. I wondered where my brothers and sisters were. They were never this quiet. I strained to hear the sound of the traffic bustling down the street, but there was nothing. Where were the sounds of the morning breakfast being made? I didn't know and I didn't care. I was content to bathe in the stillness around me. I wanted to stay asleep and keep dreaming beautiful dreams about David.

My body slowly became more aware of its surroundings. I felt the soft cotton sheets covering me. My head rested on a down pillow and it smelled like... him. I slowly opened my eyes to an unfamiliar room, and David lay next to me with his arm propping up his head.

"Good morning, Mrs. Saltate."

I blinked for a moment and then realized where I was. I wasn't in the house I grew up in. I was in the home my new husband had built for us. I was married and —

"Oh my God, what time is it?"

"It is a little after ten," David said softly as he brushed my hair back with his free hand.

"Ten! I'm late for school." I sat up in a futile attempt to make it to school. The sheet fell to my waist revealing by naked body. I gasped and clutched at the sheet, trying to cover myself.

David sat up alongside of me. He put his arms around me and pulled me back until my bare back rested against his chest. He bent his head down to whisper in my ear, "It is okay. Sam called your school early this morning and told them you would be out for the next three or four day with strep. We have all the time we need." He began kissing my neck and melting my resolve.

"I'll need a note from a doctor to get back in," I said, resting more into his embrace.

"It is taken care of too… Mrs. Saltate." He turned my head with his hand so we could kiss.

"You keep calling me Mrs. Saltate."

"Isn't that your name?"

"Is it? I mean, it isn't *your* real name, so how can it be mine?"

"I assure you, all the paperwork is legal and can stand up in any court. You *are*, Mrs. Saltate, my wife."

"But you and Don manufactured your IDs. Did you manufacture our marriage license also?"

"We *are* married. Our license is every bit as legal in this time, as if your official government had produced it. Our wedding certificate is no different from any other married couple's."

"But we are only legally married in *this* time."

"I don't need a piece of paper to tell me you are my wife. You are my wife for all time, any time; and I'm your husband, in my heart, in my mind, and in my soul. I hoped you would feel the same way."

"I do. It's just that I'm afraid something is going to separate us."

"Nothing and no one will ever part us, I promise." He kissed me and my fears disappeared.

"I think I'm going to enjoy being Mrs. Saltate and living here with you."

"Do you like our place? I built it for you."

"It is beautiful. The living room and kitchen are a little masculine, but the bed is just perfect." I winked, smiling.

"You can change whatever you want. I gave up trying to find everything in your favorite color, so I decorated the living room and kitchen in mine. You can change anything you want though. It is your home too."

"Everything is perfect. I wouldn't change a thing. I now know why Sam had such a glow about her after she got married. You Saltate boys are pretty charming."

"Well, thank you, Mrs. Saltate."

I drifted away in thought. "I'm sure my family will never forgive me for eloping."

David's carefree attitude changed. "I talked to Sam before you woke up. She already spoke to your parents and broke the news about us."

He seemed hesitant to tell me any more.

"I'm sure they were upset," I coaxed.

"They were upset, to say the least. Sam tried to assure them it was in our plans for you to finish school, graduate, and even attend college. It didn't seem to sway them. They said they would never let me set foot in their house again. They are convinced we *had* to get married."

I turned so I could wrap my arms around David's neck to show it didn't matter what they thought.

"I don't need the approval of my family. All I need is you. Besides, I still have Samantha. She is all the family I need."

David sadly shook his head. "You can't talk to Sam about leaping. You are the only one we have told. Don decided not to tell Sam, and we have to honor that. Remember, there is a fine line between inspiration and insanity. No one would believe you anyway."

"I would never tell your secret. You can trust me."

I pulled him into a kiss. David twisted me in the sheet, lying me on my back across the bed. He pressed his body down against me and kissed me deeply.

"I was thinking I should shower and get dressed," I interrupted.

"I won't fight you for the shower. You can go first."

"We have two showerheads, so you don't have to wait." I winked and threw off the sheet, streaking to the bathroom with David fast behind me.

Chapter 13

Crackers

"Ally…Ally, love." David was whispering my name into my ear. He lay next to me in our bed, our bodies spooned together. His morning whiskers tickled me awake.

"Mmm." I opened my eyes. "It is still dark. Why are you up?"

"Don and I have some business to attend to so we decided to leave early."

"Business?" I shot to a sitting positions, still locked in David's arms. "You mean *time* business, don't you?" I was fully awake now. I twisted my body in his arms so I could see his face.

"We need money to live on. Don't worry. I'll be back home in time for dinner."

"What about the Falcon, Tom? Won't he find you, catch you, arrest you, so you can't come back to me?"

"I have had no sign of him for months. Besides, Don and I can take care of ourselves. Everything will be all right. I promise."

He kissed my forehead, pulled back the covers, and left our bed.

I'm sure he felt his kiss would reassure me, but I felt dismissed. I followed him to the bathroom.

"Where *do* we get our money? You don't have a job, at least not here in *this* time. How can you and Don afford all this?"

"Inflation," he said, jumping into the shower.

"Inflation? Isn't that a bad thing? How can you get money from that?"

David peered out from behind the shower curtain. He could see his reply irritated me. He also knew I didn't like to be placated or talked down to, so he began to explain.

"If you took all of the savings you had today and went back in time to, say, 1940, you could buy more with your dollar. If you when further back to 1900, you could buy even more. We get our money from *our* time, your future."

"So what do you do, go to the future bank to withdraw money and then bring it back here to spend? Or do you make it like you make your IDs? Am I married to a counterfeiter?"

David laughed softly. "We are still working for our money even though we don't go to work *here*. Don turns in his research papers, and I have some investments. We convert our money into precious metals like gold and silver. We bring it back from the future to here and convert it into money. It is all perfectly legal."

I sighed in relief until I realized, "But you can't go back to the future. Isn't it dangerous? Aren't you wanted?"

"Don is traveling forward. I'm traveling back." David paused to see if I understood what he was saying.

"You are going to some time before now?"

"Yes, but I'll be careful. Don't worry."

"Why do you have to go back in time? What do you need to do?"

"I can buy certain things cheaper in another time period. Where do you think we get our cars from?"

"I just assumed you bought them off the internet."

He laughed. "I went back to the early 1970s, bought my car, parked it on the spot I showed you, traveled forward, picked it up, and now it is *here*."

"I see." I was beginning to feel dizzy fathoming his explanations.

"I still have a little time before I have to meet Don. Maybe we could..." He pulled at his shirt I wore as a nightgown. "Why do you insist on wearing my shirt to bed?"

"I love your shirt. It smells like you. I feel safe and comfortable in it. I dream I have your arms around me all night long."

"You *do* have my arms around you all night long. Besides, I prefer the feeling of skin to skin." He smiled, pulling me into the shower. His made a trail of kisses from my ear, across my chin, down my neck, and to my breast.

I made a deep sigh, relaxing to his touch. Just then, a wave of nausea rushed over me. I could feel the room spinning. I pulled away from David.

"Are you alright?" David asked with concern. "What's wrong? Are you sick?"

I wanted to respond, but the queasy feeling preventing me from answering. I jumped out of the shower and ran to the sink to splash water on my face and neck. I tried to take a sip of water, but the taste of it on my tongue only made matters worse, so I spit it out.

David turned off the shower and stepped out to check on me.

"What's wrong?" he said, lightly brushing my hair away from by face.

"I don't know. It must have been something I ate, or maybe I'm coming down with the flu."

"Then I won't go today. I'll stay here and take care of you."

"No… No, you go. I'll be okay. I will probably spend the day in the bathroom with the way I feel. You can go. You made plans. I'll be okay."

"I can't leave you alone if you're sick."

"I'll be fine. Besides, Sam is home. I can sit with her."

"Are you sure?"

"I'm sure. Now go get dressed. I think I need the bathroom to myself for a few minutes."

David left, giving me some privacy. I sat on the cold bathroom floor by the toilet. I felt so strange. One minute I was sick to my stomach and the next minute I was hungry. My stomach just rocked back and forth between the two feelings, making me dizzier. I left the bathroom and laid down in bed.

David finished dressing and straightened the bed so I would be more comfortable.

"Are you sure it is okay for me to go?" He looked down at me confused and worried.

"I'll be fine. I'm going to try to rest. Maybe it will pass. If not, I'll go downstairs to Sam's. Don't worry. I won't be alone. Go. Be safe and hurry back to me."

He kissed me lightly and left.

I fell asleep on and off, but each time the feeling of nausea woke me. I decided to go downstairs to see if Sam had something to settle my stomach. I got up and pulled on a pair of jeans and left our apartment.

Sam sat at the island in the kitchen, reading the morning paper and sipping coffee. Coffee. The thought, let alone the smell, made me feel worse.

"You're up. David told me to look in on you today. He said you weren't feeling well. Too bad. I was really hoping we could spend the day shopping."

My dizziness intensified. "Do you have any seltzer water? I feel so nauseous. Just the smell of your coffee is upsetting me. I feel so weird. I'm sick to my stomach and hungry all at the same time."

Sam looked me as if try to make a diagnosis. All of a sudden, she jumped from her chair, ran to me, and said, "I know just what you need." She opened the cabinet and took out a package of saltine crackers. "Here, sit down and eat a few of these."

I desperately obeyed.

"How do you feel now?" she asked.

"The crackers seem to be helping, thank you."

"I knew it! I knew it! You are pregnant."

"Me? No… At least I don't think so."

"Sure you are. Come with me. I have an EPT test in the bathroom."

With that, Sam excitedly pulled me to my feet and dragged me to the upstairs bathroom. She handed me the test kit, speedily blurting out instructions on how to use it, and left me alone.

Robotically, I did as directed. When I was finished, I opened the door, handing her the stick.

She stared at the stick and then screamed, "It is positive. We are going to have a baby! We have to go shopping to get some baby things. Oh, I'm so excited. I wanted a baby for over a year. If I can't get pregnant, having you expecting would be the next best thing. Come on. Aunt Sammy wants to start spoiling her godchild."

"Wait, hold on. I still feel sick."

"You'll be fine. Morning sickness doesn't last all day. Take the crackers and eat one every time you feel ill. Now go get dressed and meet me at the car. Hurry!"

I knew there was no way to say no to Samantha, so I went back upstairs, washed, dressed, and met her in the garage. I carried the box of crackers like they were my lifeline. I had to admit eating the crackers did make me feel better.

Sam dragged me to every baby store within a fifty-mile radius of the house. She looked at beds, strollers, dressing tables, blankets, stuffed toys, diapers. She was completely excited and ready for a baby.

I, on the hand, could barely believe what was happening.

"What if I'm not pregnant, and this is just a false alarm?"

"I know you are, trust me. Have you thought about how you are going to tell David? Oh, I wish I could see his face when you do. I know just how you should tell him. We have to find two baby outfits, one for a boy and one for a girl, then we will wrap them up as a gift and you can give it to him when he gets home tonight. Do you want a boy or a girl?"

"Wait. Everything is going too fast. David and I haven't even talked about starting a family."

"I'm sure David would love a little girl so he could spoil and fuss over her. All dads just want girls. I know if I were pregnant, Don would love a girl."

I knew it would be unfair of me to stop Sam at this point. She was having so much fun making plans for the baby. I decided to just quietly go along. In my silence, I wondered what David would say. We had never talked about children. We made plans for me to finish school and to buy a house, but never children. I always thought we would travel in time together. A baby would make that impossible.

"Well?" Sam called and I drifted back.

"Well, what?"

"Do you want a boy or a girl?"

I thought for a moment about having David's child. The more I thought about being a mother, the more I was completely absorbed by it. I had caught Sam's hysteria.

I smiled at her and said, "A boy, I want a little boy, just like his daddy"

After that, it was easy to give into Samantha's excitement. We picked out two outfits, one for a boy and one for a girl, had the clerk gift wrap them, and we were off to the next store.

The day of shopping invigorated me. I hurried upstairs to the attic apartment once we got home. I put dinner in the oven to cook and set the table for two. I turned off the lights and lit dozens of candles, placing them around the great room. I started the fireplace even though it was July. I wanted the setting as romantic as possible when I told David. I checked to make sure everything was perfect and then waited. When I finally heard David walking up the stairs, I raced to the door and jumped into his arms as soon as he stepped in.

"I'm glad to see you are feeling better," he said with a squeeze. "You had me worried."

"I'm fine," I answered and pulled him closer to me.

He pulled my braid and we kissed. "I guess you missed me."

"I did. I hope you are hungry. I made a special dinner for us."

I pulled him into the great room. He looked around at the flickering candles and the glow of the fireplace. He wrapped his arms around my waist and pulled me back into an embrace.

"What kind of *hungry* did you have in mind?" He nuzzled his head against the side of my neck, making a trail of kisses up and down my neck, making me giggle.

"Stop that, it tickles," I said, wiggling in his arms. "We are going to have dinner first. Besides, I have a gift for you."

He sat down at the table. "A gift… Let me guess. Is it something I put on you… or take off?" he said, smiling.

"Neither," I replied as I handed him the gift box. I waited in anticipation as he tore off the paper and opened the box.

He looked down at the two little outfits and looked back up to me. The smile on his face was gone.

I began to worry.

"I'm pregnant," I said quietly.

"How is that possible?"

"David, you know how it is possible. We made love continuously all over this apartment, and we never use protection. I guess it was bound to happen."

I could see David wasn't happy about my announcement.

"I know our plans didn't include a baby now, but it will be okay. I can still register for classes in the fall. The baby isn't due until March, so I'll only have to miss the spring semester. Then, next fall, I'll go back to school full time, and Sam can watch the baby."

I searched his face, but he still looked at me coldly. With tears welling up in my eyes, I choked out, "Please, David, try to be happy."

David stood up and wiped the tears from my cheeks. He put his arms around me and held me gently.

"Just give me some time. I'll get used to the idea."

Chapter 14

Intruder

July burned into August, and August melted into September. I registered for my classes at college. For the first time in our marriage, I couldn't wait for an excuse to have some time away from David. He had not gotten used to the idea of having a baby. The air between us was different… colder. Sure David acted polite, kind, and, at times, even romantic, but he always seemed pensive and distant. At first I thought he felt the baby would be an intruder to our lives, but the more I tried to reassure him, the more distant he became. I looked forward to feeling the baby move for the first time. Maybe if David could feel how real this baby was, he could fall in love with it also.

I spent more time with Samantha than David. At least I could share my excitement with someone. David, on the other hand, found a multitude of reasons to stay away from me. His time travel excursions became more frequent. He never told me where or *when* he was going. I didn't ask. I was afraid he might have found someone else in another time and was planning on leaving me, but he always came back.

One morning, David left on another one of his leaps before I woke. I felt lonely and abandoned as I sat alone in our attic apartment waiting for his return. Time seemed to stop for me whenever he left. I went downstairs, and this time I dragged Samantha on a shopping expedition. We spent the entire day together, but I reluctantly let her go. She had a husband desperate to spend time with her.

I returned to the empty attic apartment and waited. I heard the knob of the front door turning. I jumped up and rushed to meet him.

"Hello. I missed you." I wrapped my arms around his waist and squeezed. David silently squeezed back and then unlocked my arms and moved into the great room.

"Are you hungry? I can make you something to eat?"

"I ate."

"Oh," I said. He was still in his same pensive mood.

I tried to respond more enthusiastically, hoping to pull him out of his trance.

"I can't wait to show you all the things Sam and I bought today."

He just stood in the center of the room, his eyes canvassing it as if he were searching for something.

"Are you looking for something?" I questioned.

"No… Just trying to remember where everything is."

"David, are you alright? I know you have been leaping a lot lately. Does it affect your memory?" I was beginning to wonder if his increased time traveling wasn't the reason for his mood.

My question succeeded in bringing him back to the present.

"I'm fine," he said looking at me. "Show me what you and Sam bought."

"It can wait. You look tired. Maybe we should just go to bed."

"That's a good idea. I could use some sleep. I'm going to shower first. I'll see you in bed."

David robotically walked away, leaving me standing alone in the great room.

I heard the shower running while I turned off the lights and walked into the bedroom. I stared at our bed and had a flash of an idea. I hurried, pulled the covers off the bed, and threw some extra pillows on it. I turned the lights off in the room and lit some candles, placing them around the room. Finally, I changed into one of the seductive nightgowns David always gave me.

I heard the shower turn off. I jumped on the bed, nestling myself seductively into the pillows, and waited for David to emerge from the bathroom.

He opened the door. The light from the bathroom blazed into the bedroom in sharp contrast to the soft candlelight. I squinted against the light to look at him. David just stood frozen in the doorway staring at me. He turned off the bathroom light, walked to the bed, lifted the covers resting on the floor, and placed them back on the bed. He blew out the candles and laid down with his back toward me, saying nothing.

I decided to try one more act of seduction in hopes of arousing David. I spooned my body against his back and began to kiss his ear, moving to his neck. I continued my trail of kisses to his shoulder and pulled at him until he lay on his back. I continued to kiss his bare chest, then his stomach. His stomach muscles quivered in response to my lips. His hands reached for my face, and he guided me up to his. He wrapped his fingers into my hair and kissed me deeply. I could feel my body relaxing against him in a familiar interlocking. His kiss was hungry and full of desire. I surrendered completely to our sexual waltz, and then—he stopped.

He pulled away from me and said, "Good night."

I quaked against the shockwave running through me. Why was he acting like this? I thought of a hundred reasons all blurred into one twisting thought, but only one reason floated to the top: the baby. He must me worried about hurting the baby. I pressed my face against the side of his and whispered in his ear, "It is alright. I asked my doctor. We can make love. It won't hurt the baby."

"Let's not take any chances," he said, not even turning to look at me. "Now get some sleep."

Rejected, I rolled over into my space of the bed. I could feel tears welling up in my eyes. I tried to steady my breathing long enough to say, "I love you."

"I love you, too," he dutifully responded.

We laid still and silent next to one another in the dark. I wondered if this was the way it would be for us from now on. An ice-cold feeling of abandonment made me pull the covers more tightly around me. I buried my face into my pillow and let my tears flow silently. I didn't want David to know how deeply he had hurt me.

I woke the next morning to find David gone again. Not being able to take another day of isolation, I decided to dress and go downstairs to Sam's. Sam was the answer to an unsaid prayer. She always greeted me bubbling and full of excitement about the baby. It was impossible to not catch her enthusiasm.

I was still getting dressed when Samantha walked into the attic apartment.

"Morning, Ally," Sam said, walking around like she belonged here.

"I wish you would knock. David and I could still be in bed."

"I'm not that insensitive. I know he left already. Where does he keep going?"

"I don't know where he goes." That was true. I also didn't know what time drew him from me. I wish I could share that part of my life with Sam, but I had promised Don not to tell her or anyone about their ability to time travel.

"My theory is David took a second job to help pay for things now that the baby is coming. I hope the two of you aren't worried about money. I talked to Don, and we will be happy to help out."

"No, David doesn't have a second job. I guess he just needs to be alone."

"Why would he need to be alone that much? It doesn't make sense."

"I'm worried, Sam. David has been very cold and distant lately. I don't think he likes the idea of having a baby."

"That's crazy. I'm sure he is looking forward to being a daddy. It is probably just the thought of the extra responsibility that scares him. Don't worry about it so much. He'll come around."

"I hope you are right." Samantha's reassurance seemed to comfort me.

Changing the subject, Samantha said, "Okay, on our list of things to accomplish today: Where *is* this baby going to sleep?"

"I guess I'll just put a crib in our room."

"You just can't put a crib in anywhere. The baby needs his or her own space, and you and David also need your privacy. I don't want any excuses from the two of you about making more babies," she joked.

"I don't think you have to worry about more babies, at least not for a while. Let's just get this baby here," I half-heartedly replied. I felt in my heart there would never be any more babies if David remained aloof.

"Come with me to the bedroom, and let's see what we can work out."

Sam pulled me from my thoughts and into the bedroom.

"Do we have to decide today? The baby isn't due for another six months."

"We have to decide in the next hour, so let's get busy."

"Why do we have to decide in the next hour?" I asked cautiously.

"Because the furniture I ordered is being delivered."

"Sam, are you going to buy everything this baby will need for the first five years of his life before he is even born?"

"He. You said he. Do you think it's a boy?"

"I wouldn't care one way or the other. I just want a healthy baby." *I would also like a husband who is excited about the baby*, I thought. But I didn't voice my concerns.

Sam surveyed our bedroom. "We are going to have to move the bed to the wall closest the door. That will free up the other side of the room. We can put the crib there and the dresser next to it. I think the changing table might fit on the wall next to the bathroom door. What do you think?"

"I think you are totally obsessed with my baby."

"You might be right." She started knocking on the vacant wall of our bedroom. "I wonder if there is any space behind this wall. David could open it up and put in a door, and then the baby would have his own room."

"Sam, please slow down. First, I don't think *we* should be moving any furniture. Well, at least not me, in my condition. Secondly, I don't think David would like you drilling holes into the walls."

"Relax. I have movers coming to move the furniture, and I can call a contractor to remove the wall."

"Okay, I surrender. Do whatever you want," I laughed.

The movers arrived with the furniture. Samantha helmed the transformation. The work took most of the day, but when she was finished, I had to admit, the room looked perfect.

The crib she bought must have been custom made. It had four posters matching the ones on our bed. In fact, each piece of baby furniture was made of the same rich oak as the pieces already in the room. In typical Samantha fashion, she had a coverlet made for the crib matching our bed quilt identically.

When she was finished with the last detail, she surveyed her design. Satisfied, she said, "I think I do pretty good work, if I say so myself." She turned to me and continued, "I'm going downstairs to make dinner for Don. I suggest you get ready for David. I'm so excited. I wonder what David will think of our decorating. You have to promise to tell me everything he says."

I promised while hugging her. "Thank you is never enough to say when it comes to you."

"The pleasure is all mine," she said, smiling back and bouncing out the door.

The room suddenly appeared colder in her absence. I don't think it was the room itself as much as the impending chills of David's return that froze me. I sat in the darkening great room watching the warmth of the day's sun depart, and waited.

I gave into the darkness filling the room and sat without turning on a light. Finally, the door open and David walked in. I jumped to greet him, hoping his mood had improved, but he robotically kissed me hello and walked past me.

"Do you want to see what Sam and I did today?"

I didn't wait for him to respond. I towed him into our room. Nervously I began rambling explanations for the placement of each piece of furniture. I turned to look at David hoping his reaction would be more favorable hearing my enthusiasm.

David stood expressionless. He slowly turned in a circle, searching the space as if he needed to memorize it. He then turned, walked to the closet, took out his duffle bag, and began packing.

I shocked by his movements. I tried to swallow so I could speak

"What are you doing?" I whispered.

"I can't take it any more. You got what you wanted from me, so I'm leaving. I hope you'll be very happy."

"You're leaving?"

My question succeeded in igniting the emotions David kept in check. "Yes, I'm leaving," he screamed back.

"Why?"

"Why? Did you think I wouldn't find out?"

"Find out what? I don't understand."

"No, you don't understand. How stupid do you think I am? All I want to know is, *who* is the father of this baby?"

The shock of his words consumed me. "You are," I forced, barely able to speak.

"I suppose you never asked yourself why we never used protection. Why, do you think Sam isn't pregnant?"

"I… I guess I never really thought about it."

"No, I bet you didn't," he said sarcastically. "Population is out of control in the twenty-third century, so all babies are sterilized at birth. Now do you understand? I could never father a baby. Don can't give Sam one either. That is why she hasn't gotten pregnant. And you, my dear, *faithful* wife, you must have slept with someone else or you wouldn't be pregnant now."

I shook my head in disbelief. "David, you know it has only been you. There is no one else. Only you, always."

"Please," he said in disgust. He finished stuffing some clothes into the bag and turned to leave the apartment.

"No, don't leave me," I pleaded, grabbing at his sleeve in an effort to stop him.

He turned to stare at me with ice-blue eyes. "Get your hands off me."

I let go. He opened the door and started down the stairs. I knew this may be my last chance to stop him. I knew if I let him walk out of my life, I would cease to exist.

Desperately, I reached for his arm. Placing one hand around his arm and one on his shoulder, I attempted to turn him to face me. He exploded in rage and pushed me off my feet. I expect to fall backward against the stair rail, but instead I fell over it. Time seemed to stop. The ceiling was no longer above me but in front to me. I looked helplessly at David's shocked face as it seemed to move farther away from me.

I hit the landing below with a bang. A jolt of pure pain exploded in my head. I could barely hear anything other than the ringing in my ears. I felt warm liquid pooling around me and knew it must be my own blood. I stared into David's blue eyes, unable to move or speak. Everything seemed washed in a blue filter of light. I closed my eyes, hoping to end the torturous pain engulfing me.

"Ally, Ally, can you hear me?" The sound of David's voice drifted further away as I lost consciousness.

Chapter 15

Finished

"Allyson, Allyson, can you hear me? Open your eyes."

I heard a loud, unfamiliar voice. Someone was screaming at me, someone female, but it wasn't Sam.

"Allyson, open your eyes."

I tried to respond to the strange voice yelling at me, but my eyelids seemed impossibly heavy. I lay flat on my back with my arms at my sides. I remembered falling. I moved my fingers, feeling a cotton sheet under me. *How did sheets get to the wooden landing?* I wondered. I took a deep breath. The smell of my blood had been replaced with a sharp, antiseptic one. It nauseated me.

I could feel a bright light above me, hear strange people talking, but I could not move in response. I slowly forced my eyes to open, and a strange middle-aged woman looked down at me. I knew then I was in a hospital.

She busied herself checking my IV. "Good to see you are back. You are in recovery. My name is Kailah, and I'll be your nurse while on this shift. We will be taking you to your room shortly. Your husband is waiting outside. I'll let him know you are awake and bring him in."

Bring him in? I didn't want to see David, but I was too weak to stop her.

The confusing fog filling my head was parting, leaving a flood of memories to fill the void. David was leaving me. He actually believed I had cheated on him. He never wanted to see me or the baby. The baby! Oh dear God, let the baby be okay.

David interrupted my panic when he walked into the recovery room. Nurse Kailah pulled a curtain around my bed in an effort to give David and I some privacy. I looked at David's tired, scared, tortured face.

I had to ask the question, even though I knew the answer.

"How is the baby?"

David's eyes welled with tears. He said nothing, just slowly shook his head back and forth.

I couldn't look at him. I turned my head and buried my face into the pillow to cry alone.

David touched my shoulder. "I am so sorry. I never meant for this to happen."

"Sam... I want Sam," was all I could choke out.

"Sam is waiting outside. They won't let anyone else back here but me. They will be taking you back to your room shortly. I'll make sure Sam is waiting for you there."

David rubbed my shoulder to comfort me, but I pulled myself away and coiled into a ball. I felt destroyed. My heart couldn't be broken into any more pieces. I heard David pull open the curtain and walk away, leaving me alone in my grief.

An orderly arrived wheeling a gurney, and two nurses appeared to help slide me onto it. They wheeled me down the long hall and pulled into a private room. The same three people pulled me from the gurney to my bed, covering me and leaving. I looked out the window into the black night. It looked as cold and empty as I felt.

"Ally?"

I turned to see Sam standing in the doorway. I opened my arms, and she rushed to fill them as we started to cry together. We cried until my throat ached as much as my heart.

Sam brushed the hair back from my face and wiped my tears with her fingertips. She offered me a box of tissues and then a glass of water. When she felt I was calm, she said, "What happened? I left you so you could show David the bedroom. The next thing I know, David was calling for help. I rushed to him and found you unconscious and bleeding. How did you fall?"

I wanted to hurt David and tell Sam everything. I wanted to tell her she would never have a child with Don. I wanted to tell her all about the insanity of time travel they kept from her, but all I said was, "We had a fight." I couldn't hurt Sam the way I hurt.

"What could you have possibly fought about that could cause you to fall?"

"David was leaving me." I started sobbing again. "He doesn't want to be married to me anymore. I was trying to stop him, so I grabbed his arm, and when he pulled away... I fell. Sam, the baby..." The tears drowned my ability to speak.

"I know about the baby. I spoke to your doctor, and the good news is you're okay. You can start trying to have another baby in a few months."

How could I tell her there would never be another baby? I looked into her sympathetic eyes and begged, "I want to go home."

"You will, tomorrow. You suffered a concussion when you fell. The doctors want to keep you overnight for observation. They told David he could sit with you all night, but he said no. I am going to stay with you instead, if that's all right."

I nodded, holding her hand for support. Everything was beginning to make sense to me. David was done with me and waited to leave. Staying all night would just slow him down. I resigned myself to the fact David wanted out of this marriage. I held Sam's hand tightly, changing my focus to getting well. I would think about the prospect of divorce tomorrow.

Sam was my rock, my fortress, someone I could lean on. Sam stayed with me the entire night. She was there to sign me out in the morning and drive me home. She let me press my weight against her as she pulled me from the car. Her arms wrapped around me like a shield as she guided me into the house.

I couldn't wait to leave the hospital and get home, but walking in the front door of the manor took me by surprise. I was slapped in the face with a flood of memories. The balcony where David and I first met, the pillows we laid on that night Don interrupted us, the fireplace where we said our vows: Memories of David were everywhere. They cut into me like a knife, slicing my heart into minuscule pieces.

Sam tugged at my waist. "Let me get your things, and I'll help you upstairs to your apartment."

"No, *please*, not the apartment. I couldn't bear to look at it."

"David removed all the baby things and put them in storage. It will be okay."

Sure David removed all the baby things. He was probably relieved to have the baby gone. Now all he had to do is find a way to get rid of me.

"Can I stay in your guest room, the one I used to use?"

"If that is what you want."

"I do. I just need to be alone, away from all the memories."

"I'll help you upstairs and then go to your apartment to get some of your things."

"I'll take care of that." The sound of David's voice behind me almost caused me to faint. He scooped me up in his arms, carried upstairs to the guest room, and placed me on the bed.

I noticed then his hand was bandaged. "Did you hurt yourself?"

"It is nothing. I'll get your things and be right back." David walked out of the room just as Sam was walking in.

"I brought you some tea." She handed me the cup to drink. Looking around the room, she continued, "I don't think it is a good idea for you to stay in this room alone. It is one thing to grieve, it is another thing to shut yourself off from the rest of the world. There isn't even a television in here. I think you should be with David. He really is upset about what has happened. He was so distraught he punched a hole in the wall and almost broke his hand. I'm sure you two can work this out if you would only talk to one another."

"I'll be fine. Please understand, I just need to be alone so I can sort out my feelings. I'll come downstairs to socialize as soon as I am able."

"Promise you'll call me if you need anything."

"I promise. Thank you for everything. I couldn't do this without you."

"What are sisters for?"

Sam left, and David returned with an arm full of my clothes.

"I brought you some jeans and shirts, a robe, slippers, your toothbrush, and your pillow." He hesitated. "I also brought one of my shirts to sleep in."

"You can take it back. I think I outgrew that foolishness."

Rejected, David pulled back his arm holding the shirt and left.

Being alone helped me to sort through my thoughts and feelings. The gap between David and I widened with each passing day, though Sam was forever trying to forge a bridge between us. She told me David had felt so bad about what happened, he smashed his own hand. She said she saw him break down and cry when the doctor told him about the baby.

As much as I wanted to believe there was hope of having David back in my life, he remained distant. We had to finish this standoff once and for all. I knew just what had to be done. I told Sam to get David so I could speak to him.

He quickly responded, appearing at the door of the guest room.

"You wanted to see me?"

"Yes. I have been giving our situation a great deal of thought. I can only see one logical thing to do."

I knew I had to say the next line as calmly and unemotionally as possible. I knew what I was about to say would bring a sense of relief to David, but it would kill me. If I loved David, I needed to let him go. It was the only way he could be happy, free. I mustered my strength, looked at him, and said, "I want a divorce."

"What?" His response was quiet and full of hurt, making my charade more difficult.

"There isn't any *real* reason we need to stay together. There is no baby, not that it was any concern of yours. Our marriage was counterfeit to begin with, so it should be fairly easy to make up another sheet of paper that says we aren't married."

"I told you before, our marriage *is* real."

"Well, then I want a *real* divorce."

"I'll make the arrangements. I'll pack my things and get out of the apartment by tomorrow morning."

"I don't want the apartment. You can have it."

"I built it for you."

"All the same, I decided I'm going home, back to my parents. You can mail the papers there if you want."

I stood staring at him. It took all of my strength to look as cold and uncaring as possible. I must have been convincing because he turned and left the room without another word.

I slowly walked to the door, closed it, and fell to the floor. I clasped my hands over my mouth to silence my tears. It was over. David was gone. He was taking my heart and soul with him, leaving me only the memory of him forever branded on my mind.

Chapter 16

Return

I lifelessly returned to my family's home. My parents coldly ignored me because they still hadn't forgiven me for my sudden elopement or lying to them.

I felt more like a zombie going through the motions of life, soulless. I started college and loaded myself with classes. It didn't matter how much work the classes produced, I couldn't sleep, so I had plenty of time on my hands.

When I wasn't at school, I was at home. I discovered everyone left me alone. I dutifully shared meals with my family, but we refrained from any conversation.

I saw reminders of David everywhere. He was in the sunrise, the rain, the traffic, the sunset, the moonlight, the pillow I lay on... everywhere. Each thought of him cut into me. My parents attributed my melancholia to losing the baby; but in truth, I ached more for David.

Except for the day of our divorce, I never saw or heard from David. I knew my decision to set him free was the right thing to do because he just... disappeared. He walked away, confirming my original theory: I was forgettable.

My classes finished by 1 PM every Tuesday. It was too early to return to my prison at home, so I walked to the library. There was a secluded corner on the second floor where no one ever went. It was also my new hiding place. I could work on the day's assignment, sit by the window, and gaze out watching people who were actually alive.

I had been working about an hour on one of my research papers when I decided to take a stretch break. Looking out the library window, I watched the people moving about the campus. There were men and women walking together or in groups, and I jealously observed their lively shuffling. One couple stopped to catch a quick kiss. Their intimacies only made my inside ache worsen. I watched their embrace for a moment and then turned my eyes back to the crowd.

As I scanned the people bustling below, the sight of a figure all dressed in black caught my eye. For an instant I was transported back to that day in the grocery store. Familiar fear shot through me. The stranger was stalking me again, only this time there was no David to save me. I closed my eyes, but when I opened them again, the figure in black was gone. I rationalized my hallucination, chalking it up to lack of sleep, and returned to my studies.

The library closed at four on Tuesdays, so I picked up my things and headed for the bus. As I walked I caught a glimpse of the black-clad figure again. This time he sat on a motorcycle. I stared at him, trying to keep my irrational fears in check. He wore a black leather jacket, black jeans, and boots. The bike he sat on was also black. His head was hidden under a black helmet, so I couldn't see his face. As I watched, he started the bike, circled the parking lot, and left.

The bus arrived. I shock my head, trying to dislodge the image of the stranger, and boarded the bus. I couldn't listen to my i-pod because the air-waves were filled with songs of finding or losing love, and they were too painful of a reminder. I remained in a trance, reliving the day in the market. I glanced out the window of the bus as I did on that day, and my heart skipped a beat. The black-clad motorcyclist was next to us in traffic. I began watching him more carefully just to make sure he wasn't following me. I breathed a sigh of relief when he turned off a few streets from my house.

I entered the apartment building from the back door, dredging up to the second floor. My younger brothers and sisters were racing past me as I entered, ignoring me. I thanked God for affording me the power of invisibility.

I walked through the apartment surveying the wreckage of my siblings at play. I began to pick up the toys scattered about the living room. Cutting through a jungle of mess, I reached the window seat and sat down to catch a moment to pull myself together.

I was desperately in need of sleep, but sleep escaped me. I purposely left all reminders of David locked behind in the attic apartment, but what I wished I had taken was one of David's shirts. I was certain I could sleep if I was wrapped in the essence of him, but it was too late now to retrieve one. The keys to the attic apartment were awarded to David in the divorce.

I wearily glanced out the picture window above the window seat. I gasped in horror. My heart started beating wildly. There, in front of my house, was the man in black. He sat on his motorcycle, bending down to talk to *my* little sister. I dropped the items in my hand and ran down the front stairs, leaving all the doors I passed opened. I stormed into the street to confront this stranger and to rescue my sister.

"Carrie, get into the house," I ordered. "You know you are not supposed to talk to strangers." Carrie obeyed, quickly running back through the front door. I stood fastened in place, ready for a confrontation.

The stranger looked up at me and slowly rose to his feet. I looked at him. He was about thirty, well over six feet, and muscular. His hair was jet black, and he wore a sculpted mustache and beard. He stared back at me with eyes, sapphire blue, like David's.

I didn't give him time to speak. I hit my fists into his chest and yelled, "Okay, so you are back. Take your bounty. Take me. But leave my family out of this. Go on. You want me so badly, take me."

I knew he must wear a time crystal like David's, so I tore at his black shirt trying to expose it.

He grabbed my wrists in each of his hands to restrain me. "Slow down. I'm not here to hurt you or your family, and please lower your voice. You are causing a scene."

"You want a scene? How about I start yelling everything I know about time travel?"

"They will only think you've lost your mind."

He was right. I had to calm down. I took a deep breath in the hope of gaining my composure.

"Why are you here?" I asked firmly.

"I was curious. I heard you were to have a baby in March. It is April now. Why isn't my brother here defending you? Surely he wouldn't leave you and the baby unguarded."

"David is not here, and I lost the baby."

"I… I'm so sorry."

"I bet you are. You probably hoped to get double the bounty if you took me and the baby."

"Is there somewhere were we can go? To talk? This is a bit too open."

I studied him for a moment. Maybe it was the fact that I had no one to talk to, maybe it was the fact that I didn't care what happened to me, or maybe it was the fact that he had the same true blue eyes David had that made me want to go with him. Staring at him, I said, "There is a coffee shop at the end of the block. We can go there."

He dismounted his bike, and we walked silently to the corner of the street. When we reached the coffee shop, we walked in and took a booth in the back.

"Can I get you some coffee or tea?" he asked graciously.

"I try not to *travel* on a full stomach," I said sarcastically.

"Why do you say that?"

"Aren't you here to take me to the future so you can collect your bounty?"

"I haven't taken you yet, have I?"

"Then why did you come back?"

"I know I frightened you the last time I was here, but I mean you no harm. David told me to keep away, and I did. David agreed to go back with me, but he lost me when he veered in and out of time. I wanted to know what was so compelling about you that he was willing to die in your place. I assumed he somehow made it back to you and leapt with you. I started search through time for a traveling couple. I didn't know I was on the wrong trail until Don published a paper describing the pregnancy of the first Halo. I knew then, you were still *here*. I decided to wait for you to give birth before I'd return."

"So you planned to take the baby instead of David and me?"

"That was my original plan, but the more I thought about it, the more I knew I couldn't."

"How noble of you."

"You haven't told me yet, where is David?"

"David and I are divorced."

"Divorced? I didn't think he could leave you, so you must have left him."

"Let's just say it was a mutual decision."

"So what broke the two of you up? Was it the thought of time travel?"

"I was prepared to go anywhere or any time with David. It was his lack of trust in me that tore us apart."

"At first I thought my brother must be trying to seduce you into coming with him because of the sizeable bounty, but when I heard about your baby, I knew he would stay here to raise his child."

"He didn't even believe the baby was his. He told me that everyone in the twenty-third century is sterilized at birth, therefore he couldn't be the father."

"What a fool. So you left David over that and not the idea of time travel? Did he ever try to leap with you?"

"Once, but he changed his mind. Why?"

"Did he tell you why he couldn't take you to our time?"

"No."

"You are a Halo, *the* Halo."

"He told me that but didn't explain much more."

"Halos are the only people in the twenty-third century allowed to procreate. Halos can use their minds to see into the souls of others or to see if a soul even exists. The hope of the government is to strengthen the Halo gene in people by producing a more advanced race of humans, humans with the ability to manipulate matter, time, and even other humans with their minds. If a female is found having the gene, like you, they are forced to be inseminated and become breeders of future humans. David knew your fate if you were captured. He couldn't let you become a prisoner, so he kept you to himself for protection. He couldn't let you live the life of a captive Halo."

"If he loved me so much, how could he believe I would cheat on him?"

Tom laughed.

"What's so funny?" I said, infuriated.

"That stupid brother of mine. Did he ever stop to think who provided the sperm for the Halo breeding program? The halos can't impregnate themselves."

"Where *do* the donors come from?"

"Every child born in my time is DNA tested at birth. The females containing the Halo gene are placed in a secluded location where they are raised until they are old enough to bear children. Males can also carry the Halo gene, but it is unusual. If a male is found having the gene, he is not sterilized. His records are marked 'donor,' and he is left to live his life until his sperm is harvestable."

"Then David is a donor? Why didn't he know about this?"

"David must have leapt in time before he was notified."

I sat thinking how differently my life would be in contrast to the reality of what it was if only David had this information.

"It doesn't matter. David is long gone. I don't know where or even when he is."

"He does leap quickly in and out of time. He is very hard to track, let alone catch."

I nodded as more hope of David's return was taken from me.

"So now what?"

"I would very much like the privilege of knowing you."

"Knowing me? Don't you want to take me back and collect the bounty?"

"I'm not tracking you nor am I here to take you back."

"Then why did you come back?"

"You fascinate me. I've never met a Halo before. According to the papers Don published, you have the ability to see deeply into the souls of others. I guess I'm curious to find out if I even have a soul. Do you think we can at least be friends?"

I looked deeply into his eyes and felt he was trustworthy. Confidently I said, "Yes. But... my parents are going to have a problem with the age difference between us. What are you, about thirty?"

Tom laughed out loud.

"I'm thirty-three. And as for the age difference, you are two hundred years older than me.

Chapter 17

Restore

Spring had finally arrived, and the sun washed the world in hope and light; but I felt desolate. One year ago today, David and I eloped. I would have never imagined observing this day without him; yet here I was, alone.

I walked into the school library at the end of class just to hide in my secluded spot by the window. I sat down at my usual seat and stared out. How could I make it through another day without him, let alone *this* day?

I surveyed the grounds below from my perch. It was then I noticed Tom standing there. He looked up at the window and, seeing me, bade me to come down. Astounded, I obeyed.

"What are you doing here?" I asked a bit bewildered.

"I couldn't let you go through this day alone, could I?"

"How do you know what day this is?"

"I know everything about you. I've read all the papers ever written about you. You are very well known in the twenty-third century."

"Really? Why am I so famous?"

"You are the source, the origin, of the Halo gene. Human beings were corrupt until your mutated gene was discovered. There wasn't anything written about you until David found you, and Don started publishing his papers. You probably wouldn't be famous, but they changed the future by their actions here, in this time."

He must have see the confusion his words caused me, so he finished, "Enough. I came to take you for a ride on this beautiful spring day, not to talk about the time-space continuum."

"Where are we going?"

"I thought I would take you for a ride on my bike."

"I've never been on a bike."

"Then, my dear, you have never lived."

He scooped his arm around my waist and pulled me to where his bike was parked.

He took off his jacket, draped it around my shoulders, and said, "Here, put this on. I don't want you catching a cold."

He must have seen how his gesture caused me to freeze and shut down. "What's wrong? What did I say to upset you?" he asked concerned.

"It is not you. It is your jacket. It smells like David."

"So, he has good taste in cologne as well as women," he joked, making light of my response. "Here, I got you a helmet."

"It is blue! Did you also know that blue is my favorite color?"

"No, but I do now." He helped me on the back of the motorcycle and then got on himself.

I leaned back to avoid touching him, but the seat forced us closer.

"You have to put your arms around my waist," he said over his shoulder.

I reluctantly made a circle around his waist with my arms, and we were off. The power and speed of the bike forced me to hold him tighter. Resting my head against his back was the only comfortable way to sit. At first I felt like I shouldn't be doing this with him, but the more we drove, the more comfortable I became.

He had complete control over the bike and me. He made a roller coaster of our ride by jumping small hills. The rise and falls made butterflies in my stomach and, for the first time in nearly a half a year, I laughed.

Time seemed to stop. Before I knew it, we returned to the campus parking lot, and my adventure was over.

Tom helped me off the bike and took off my helmet. He smiled and said, "Well, at least I restored your smile. You have a very pretty smile. You should wear it more often."

"Thank you. I needed to do something to make me feel alive. When can we go for a drive again?"

"How about a picnic on Saturday?"

"I would like that."

"I'll pick you up at your house at 11?"

"It is a date."

A date? Did I just make a date with another man? I thought how I still felt about David and decided this thing between Tom and I would just be a friendship. I would not let myself be hurt again.

It took forever for Saturday to arrive. The slow passage of time was compounded by the fact I still could not sleep without David. I left the marriage with nothing, but there wasn't a day that went by that I would not have gladly traded anything for one of his shirts to sleep in.

I busied myself on Saturday morning, packing a lunch and blanket for the picnic. I showered, dressed, and put on my jean jacket, making sure I was ready by ten. I decided to wait for Tom in front of the house to avoid the scrutiny of my family. They still hadn't forgiven me for eloping with David. I could just image their wrath in meeting Tom.

My body ached from lack of sleep. My head pounded as I paced up and down in front of the house, waiting. I was beginning to feel forgotten when Tom pulled up, restoring my faith.

He placed my bag of food in one compartment of his bike and the blanket in another. He handed me my helmet, lifted me on to the back of his bike, and sat down. I eagerly wrapped my arms around him this time, resting my head comfortably against his back, and we were off.

Tom chose a secluded spot in a forest preserve outside of the city for our picnic. He parked the bike, and we walked to a shaded area. It felt comfortable to be with Tom. I looked forward to spending the day with him, but my headache pounded to a point of distraction.

"What is wrong? Did my driving make you nauseous?"

"No. I have this terrible headache. I've been having trouble sleeping since… you know… since David left. I guess I should have called the picnic off, but I didn't know how to reach you."

"I'm glad you didn't. Here, let me help you."

Tom sat behind me on the blanket and began messaging the back of my neck, moving to my shoulders, and then my back.

I was hesitant for him to touch me so intimately, but his therapeutic touch was impossible to resist.

"Just try to relax. You're so tense," he said, massaging.

After a few minutes, I gave into his touch and gave a deep sigh of relief.

"You can lean back and take a nap if you like."

"I can't sleep here! We are supposed to be on a picnic."

"I didn't take you out to be entertained. If you need to sleep, sleep."

Tom lay on his back on top of the outstretched blanket and opened his arms to me. His gesture shocked me. He was expecting me to lay down with him, in his arms, with him as my pillow.

I stopped for a moment to look him in his eyes. I saw a calm tenderness reflecting back, so I submitted to his request, lying my head against his shoulders.

He wrapped me in his arms, comforting me with the warmth of his body. I closed my eyes, breathing in his cologne—David's cologne, the scent I longed for, the scent I missed. He gently continued his massaging of my neck, shoulders, and back while I drifted into sleep.

I slept peacefully. Still lost in my sweet dreams, I moved my hands, tracing the familiar outline of David's body. I took in a deep breath to fill my lungs with the scent of him. I nestled my face against his chest. I felt the familiar tug on my braid and responded by bending my head back. I felt his lips warm against mine as electricity raced through my body. I moved my hand to his face and wound my fingers into his golden hair. The kiss deepened, and I ran my hand down his face, feeling his beard— beard?

Oh my God, I was kissing Tom not David. The shock of my action woke me fully, and I jumped to a sitting position.

"I shouldn't have done that," I said to Tom in horror.

"It's alright. I knew you were kissing him and not me."

"It just that you... pulled my braid."

"I'm sorry. Did I hurt you?"

"No... It is just, David used to pull my braid. It was our way of... kissing." I could feel the tears beginning to flow.

"What the *hell* did he do to you?" Tom sat up in concern and took my face in his hands. "If he decided to leave you, great; but did he have to leave you utterly destroyed like this?"

"I'll be alright. I just have to get over him, that's all."

"Get over him? How? He left you just a shell of yourself. How are you possibly going to get over him?"

"You're right. I have to force myself to move on. My heart and soul will always belong to David, but there is no hope of him ever returning. I have to find a way to keep going."

"I'll help, if you let me." Tom tenderly stroked the side of my face, wiping the tears away with his thumb.

"I think I would like that."

"Then we will make a pact to forget about *him*. Shall we eat?"

Tom began to pull things from the bag I packed.

I put my hand on his arm to get his attention.

"Tom, can I ask you something?"

"Sure, anything."

"Can I have one of you shirts to sleep in?"

"You want it because it smells like him, don't you?"

"Yes," I said softly, embarrassed.

"I don't think it is a good idea, but I'll give you the one I'm wearing when I bring you home today. I don't want to be blamed for you not sleeping." He teasingly threw a grape at me and smiled.

"Oh, Tom, what would I ever do without you?"

Chapter 18

Reunite

Tom called and said he would be picking me up in thirty minutes. I had become used to his last-minute requests. He instructed me to look nice and hinted we were going some place special.

Tom was unlike David, and the difference served me well. Tom never came anywhere near my family, unlike David who easily fit in. Tom was wild, crazy, and light. David was mesmerizing, smoldering, and addictive. Tom was enjoyably comfortable; and with Tom, I was learning to live without David.

I dressed quickly, putting on a pair of my best jeans and a white, ruffled, cotton shirt. I grabbed my jean jacket also. It may have been a nice spring evening, but the back of Tom's bike was always chilly. I hurried downstairs to greet Tom.

"Let me see what you are wearing," he said upon first seeing me.

I opened my jacket and turned around slowly to model my choices. Tom looked me over and then reached to unbutton the top three buttons of my shirt. The act of him partly undressing me caused me to gasp. Tom and I were just friends, and this intimate of a connection made me feel uncomfortable.

"Why did you do that?" I asked.

"I want everyone to be jealous of what I got."

"But you don't *have* me, at least not like that."

"No one at the party has to know we are just friends. I want everyone to think you're my date, okay?"

"I guess so. Did you say party? What party? Where are you taking me?"

"You'll see when we get there. Hop on."

I obeyed but silently wondered where we were going. I never asked Tom what he did when he wasn't with me. I guess I would find out now.

We drove for a while and then pulled up in front of a townhouse. I could hear music and the sounds of the people talking coming from the inside. Tom dismounted the bike, took my hand, and we started for the door.

Something just didn't feel right about me pretending to be his date, so I hesitated.

"I don't know about this. I'm not in a partying mood," I said, pulling him back by his arm.

"It's okay. We can leave anytime you want to." He scooped his arm around my waist and pulled me to the door, ringing the bell.

The door opened, revealing a house packed with people. They all looked to be in their twenties, so I knew this was more like a frat party than a family reunion. Tom slid his arm from around my waist so he could take my hand and lead me through the sea of people. He greeted some of them by name as he pulled me deeper into the house.

"Hello. Surprised to see me?"

I heard him greet someone, but I was hidden behind his back and couldn't see who it was. "I want you to meet my date."

Tom pulled me to his side, and I looked up and stopped breathing.

It was David. He stood on the other side of the makeshift bar with a cute Asian girl at his side.

"Oh, wait. You already know my date, don't you, brother?" Tom sounded cold and menacing. "Don't want to talk? That's alright." Tom turned his attention away from David and to the Asian girl. "Who might you be, my lovely?"

"Hi, my name is Beti," she said, offering her hand to shake.

Tom reached to hold her hand, saying, "I'm Tom, David's half-brother, and this is my date, Ally."

I nodded hello and looked at her more carefully. She smiled sweetly back at me. I then glanced over to David only to be met with a cold, contained glare.

David looked at Tom like he was ready to kill him. Tom disregarded David's impending fury and spoke directly to Beti.

"I heard congratulations were in order, Beti."

Beti stretched out her left hand in response to show off the sparkling diamond ring on her finger. She smiled contently and leaned against David.

"David just surprised me with the ring yesterday. Isn't it perfect?"

She was engaged to David!

"You have excellent taste in women, brother."

I couldn't bear the way David kept looking at me or the sight of Beti's flashing diamond beacon. I turned to search the room for any hope of an exit, but the crowd blocked any possibility of leaving, so I found a place to sit adjacent to the bar. I wanted to just disappear, but there was no way of leaving, so I sat horrified, listening as the conversation continued.

David spoke in a low, controlled voice to Tom, but his fury was still evident.

"What are you doing here?"

"I came to share in your joy. Let's drink to your future happiness. I'll have two beers, that way my date can toast you too."

"Ally doesn't drink."

Totally disregarding David, Tom took two beers off the bar.

"She does a lot of things with me. We are really very close. We even slept together."

Tom turned and walked to where I was sitting.

"Here, have a drink. You look like you need one."

I shook my head no, but Tom forced the beer bottle into my mouth. I tried to swallow, but the beer flowed faster than I could drink and poured down my neck, saturating my shirt. I looked at Tom hurtfully.

"Why are you doing this to me? Why did you bring me here?"

"It's time you stopped mourning this dead love of yours."

"Did you have to tell him we slept together?" I looked at him, astounded by his audacity.

Tom didn't answer. He kept looking over my shoulder to monitor David's reaction. He then grabbed me by my braid, forcing my head back. He leaned forward, thrust his tongue deep into my mouth, and pressed down against me roughly.

I couldn't breathe. I pushed at him to let me go, but he pressed down harder. Unable to control him, I waited motionless for my release. When I was finally freed, my tears began to flow.

"Can you please take me home?" I begged.

"You want to go? Then go," he said, ignoring my request and returning to his beer.

I felt like everyone was looking at me. Ashamed, I stoically stood up. Holding in my tears, I walked to the door and left. I didn't know which way to walk, and I didn't care. I just wanted to get as far away from the townhouse as possible. I staggered in an effort to run. Sobs and gasps choked from my mouth uncontrollably.

I ran without direction, managing to put several blocks between me and the townhouse. I stopped briefly to catch my breath and assess my surroundings. I had no idea where I was or how to get home. I crumbled to the ground and sat on the cold sidewalk, reviewing what had just happened. I had stopped living when David left, but I always held the hope in my heart he would come back to me. In truth, David didn't miss me at all. He had moved on and found someone else.

Tom, who I thought was my friend, was really using me just to torment his brother. My life couldn't get any more messed up then I already had made it. It was then I saw David's yellow convertible coming toward me. I pulled myself to my feet and began running. I should have realized I could never outpace the car.

David pulled up next to me and shouted, "Get in."

I just kept walking, praying either he or I would disappear.

"You are going the wrong way," David called.

I stopped. I thought for a moment and decided a ride from David, no matter how painful, would at least get me home. I turned and got into his car, sitting as close to the passenger door as possible. I tried, in vain, to keep myself composed, but my tears kept flowing. Lost in my own thoughts and tears, I hadn't notice the car stopping. I looked up to see Sam and Don's house.

"Why did you bring me here?" I asked.

"Don't you live here?"

"No, I live with my parents."

"Why? I cleared out my things. The place is yours."

"I couldn't live where we…" The few raw emotions I held in check burst forward, and I broke down, dissolving into hysterics. I sobbed in gasps, hiccupping out words in between.

"Oh, David, I made such a mess out of my life."

"You didn't do it alone." The soft tone in David's voice surprised me. It was soft, comforting, and familiar. He gently brushed back my hair and dried my tears with the back of his fingers. Staring at me he said, "This is the most surreal moment of my life. It reminds me of the night I took you home. Do you remember, the night Don walked in on us? You were crying like you are now. All I wanted to do was comfort you… just like I do now."

I threw myself at David, saying, "David, don't leave me."

He wrapped me in his familiar embrace and said, "If I stay, I'll want to be more… do more… than just be a shoulder to cry on."

I didn't care what happened next. I pulled him into a kiss.

He warmly responded, pulling me tightly against his body. He kissed my lips, cheeks, and forehead until my tears stopped.

I knew we couldn't spend the night in the car, so I said, "I don't have any keys to our apartment, and I really don't want to talk to Sam right now. What should we do?"

"Open the glove compartment. I have a set."

I took out the keys and looked at David. I could see he wanted to be with me as much as I wanted to be with him.

He took my hand, and we walked quietly into the back door and stole up the stairs to our apartment. He unlocked the door, and we walked into the darkened space. Once David had led us into the bedroom, he pulled the dusty cover from the bed, rolled it up, and threw it on the floor.

I interrupted our reunion, saying, "I'm going to have to wash up. I smell like beer." After receiving his nod in reply, I went to the bathroom, quickly undressed, and jumped into the shower. When I was finished, I pulled back the curtain to see David standing there holding an open the towel. Flashes of our wedding night flooded back as I moved to him. He folded me into the towel, lifted me into his arms, and walked to the bed. All the hurt, loneliness, and doubt disappeared. We were together, and that was all that mattered. We surrendered to our emotions, dancing in the sheets, reunited as one.

Chapter 19

Reason

I opened my eyes and looked around. I was home in our attic apartment, and I sighed with deep contentment. I turned my head to see David's beautiful face calmly sleeping next to me. Resting on my elbow, I lightly brushed his wayward blond hair from his forehead. I felt like I must be dreaming. Was he really here? Mine again? Moved, I kissed his forehead, and his eyes blinked awake in the morning sunlight.

"Good morning, Mr. Saltate."

David studied his surroundings for a moment and then said, "Beti!" He jumped to his feet, throwing off the sheet. With hurried movements, he dressed, quickly pulling on his boxers and jeans in one flowing movement. He stepped into his shoes, grabbed his shirt, and ran to the front door of the apartment, slamming it closed behind him.

I had expected him to wish me good morning, cuddle maybe. I never expected him to call the name of another girl and rush back to her. What had happened last night between us? Was it all some kind of a game David played? The more I reviewed the events of last night, the more used and dirty I felt. I ran to the shower and brushed vigorously in an attempt to scrub away the feeling of rejection. I let the water pour over me until it ran cold, then I turned off the shower and dressed. I wanted to cry, but no tears came. I was in shock. How could David use me like this and just leave?

I decided it was time I take charge of my life. I sat down at the kitchen table and took inventory of my options. I was eighteen and had a lot of time left to live, but I would have to live it alone. I had been married, but now it was over. I had almost had a child, but my husband didn't believe it was his. I had found my one true love, but he had broken my heart. As much as David had hurt me though, I still loved him. And with that thought, my tears began to flow.

I cried until my face was red and my throat burned. I needed someone to help bind the pieces of my heart together so it could go on beating, but who could I turn to? Samantha. I could count on her to give me advice. I washed my face and ran downstairs to find her.

I called Samantha's name out to announce I was in her kitchen, but there was no answer. I began searching the house, checking every room on the first floor, but to no avail. It wasn't like Samantha to leave and not tell someone or leave a note. I walked to the second floor, exploring further, but nothing. I finally checked her bedroom, only to find an unmade bed and clothes lying on the floor. If Don and Samantha left, it must have been in a hurry. Why would they leave so abruptly? She didn't know anything about the crystals, spores, Halos or time travel; but the feeling they needed to flee quickly worried me.

I heard someone walking back into the house through the back door and rushed to it in hopes it was Samantha and I was just a victim of an overactive imagination.

David greeted me. "What? You looked surprised to see me."

"I am."

"Why? I thought after last night, things between us were settled. Now what?"

"Well, forgive me if I act surprised. I guess I wasn't properly prepared to have you call out another woman's name. You just jumped out of our bed and ran to her."

"What did you want me to do, break the engagement over the phone?"

"You broke off the engagement?"

"Yes, the law frowns on having two wives."

"We're not married, remember?"

"I've been thinking about that. I think you should plan our next wedding since I planned the first one."

"How do I know you won't run off and leave me again?"

"You don't. You just have to trust me."

"Like you trust me?"

"I was wrong. It doesn't matter whose baby it was. I feel terrible that I was the cause of your to losing it."

"So you still think I could cheat on you. Tom explained it to me. He says you are stupid."

"Does he? How so?"

"You see, he told me all about the Halo breeding program. Do you know how a Halo gets pregnant?"

"They are inseminated."

"Then who are the donors if everyone is sterilized at birth?"

David stopped to digest what I just said.

"I am a donor? Oh my God, the baby... It was mine. Can you ever forgive me?"

"I love you, that is all that matters."

I reached for David. He wrapped his arms around me and kissed me. He rested his head on the top of mine and said, "Let's find Sam and Don and start planning our wedding. I can't wait another minute."

Their names pulled me back to my original state of panic. "I searched the house for them. They are not here. It looks like they had to leave in a hurry. David, I'm worried."

"It is not like Don to just leave. I agree something must be wrong. There is only one reason I know that would cause Don to leave in a rush without a word. A falcon must have found them."

"A falcon? Tom is a falcon. You don't think he could have taken them? Please, David, I know you don't like him, but we have to find out what happened. Can you call Tom?"

"Falcons are trackers. You don't call them. They find you. If a falcon did take Sam and Don, he will be back for us. We will just have to wait here. Tom will show up."

"How long do we have to wait?"

"I can try to travel forward to the future to see if I can find anything out, if you like."

"No, don't leave me."

I tightened my body to his with my arms. If a falcon was coming, these may be the last minutes we had together.

"All right, then we just sit and wait."

The day drifted into night. I could tell David was just as worried I as was, but he never shared any of his theories about what may have happened to Sam and Don.

It was just before ten when we heard a knock on the back door. David got up to open it with me following closely behind.

There stood Tom.

"You have to get out of here. They sent a flock of falcons to find you. It's just a matter a time." Tom looked over David's shoulder to see me. "I'm glad my little act woke the two of you up, and you are together again."

David ignored the comment and asked, "It's because of the bounty that they want us, isn't it? But why send a flock to get me? One falcon could do the job. *You* could do the job"

"You, dear brother, are no more than an irritant, a spore. She, on the other hand, is more valuable; and together, the two of you are dangerous."

"How can we be a threat?"

"Separately, you mean nothing; but together…" Tom shook his head back and forth. "Together you are the beginning of a new race of people. Your children will be able to control things, other humans, and time with their minds alone. The government can't let the two of you multiply, so a flock was sent to capture both of you."

"How did they find us? Did you tell them where we were?"

"No. Don did."

"Don?"

"Every time he published a paper reporting on Ally, another piece was exposed. At first they thought the source was Don and his wife, but after reviewing Don's medical records and his papers on his wife, they ruled him out. It wasn't until he published the paper about Ally being pregnant that everything exploded. They checked your medical records and compared them to Ally's, and that confirmed their suspicions. Together, you were the source. They increased the bounty in hopes of capturing you both. A flock of falcons arrived a few days ago but mistakenly took Don and his wife for you two."

"Oh, no," I gasped.

"They are alright. I got here first and convinced them to leap. I think I covered their tracks, so I don't believe anyone can follow them. We shouldn't waste any more time talking. There are falcons on your trail, and they should be here soon."

"Why should we trust you?"

"You have no reason to trust me, but Ally does. I don't care what happens to you, little brother, but I can't stand by and see her captured without doing something."

David turned to pull me to his side. "Then we will leap, and hopefully they won't be able to find us."

"Leaping is a great idea, but she can't leap with you," interjected Tom.

"She doesn't leave my side."

"Come on, Dave, be reasonable. Your crystal is designed to carry one. Mine, on the other hand, is designed to carry two. She will be safer with me."

"I don't trust you."

"I don't care if you trust me. *She* trusts me."

"You'll be wanted and disgraced if they catch you helping us. Why would you jeopardize yourself like that?"

"I told you, I care for her too. I don't want anything to happen to her I could prevent. Enough talking. We have to get going. Time is running out."

David turned to me. "Tom is right. It is safer to leap with him."

I shook my head no and tightened my hold on David, unable to speak.

"We will leap at the same time. I'll be right behind you. I promise."

"What if something happens and we lose each other? I can't live without you," I said, my head spinning with fear.

"I will always find you, no matter where or when you are. Now go with Tom."

David peeled my arms from around his waist and pushed me into Tom's waiting hands. I shook my head in disbelief, unable to comprehend what was happening.

Tom exposed the onyx-colored crystal he wore around his neck. "It will be safer if you hold the crystal and I hold you," he instructed me.

I looked at David. I'm sure he could feel the fear I felt nauseating me. I could see the same fear in his face.

"I'll be right behind you. You have nothing to worry about. I'll see you on the other side," he said trying to reassure me.

"What if something goes wrong?"

"Nothing will go wrong. Tom will protect you, and I *will* find you. You are my love, my life, my destiny. I can't, I won't exist without you." He kissed me through my tears and pushed me against Tom's chest.

I swallowed and said, "I love you."

Closing my fingers around the crystal, Tom engulfed me in his arms and we leapt.

Chapter 20

Awake

I awoke incoherent and disorientated.

Ever since my first leap, years ago, I had always been in control. I would pick a time, place, or event, concentrate while holding the Saltanium crystal firmly, and leap. My landings were certain and precise, no surprises. It was as if I focused on a certain spot, jumped from a height, and landed on my feet. I had maybe thirty or more leaps to my credit, but this leap felt different.

This time my landing was skewed. A wave of panic rushed over me. For a moment, I wanted to stand and run directionless, wildly, but giving in to the panic would do me no service. I decided instead to assess my surroundings before making my next move.

Firstly, I needed to remember where I was before I leapt. I was certain I would not have jumped from the position I now found myself in. I was lying on my back on some sort of a bed. I would never leap so casually as to lie down to do it. Just one more reason why this leap felt wrong.

I strained to remember where I was and what I was doing just before my leap. It took all my effort to see through my clouded memories. As the fog in my head began to clear, I visualized the interior of an old Victorian manor. A dark, moonless night shed no light on the space I occupied.

I noticed a single candle burning on a table. I concentrated on the flickering flame in my mind and let it illuminate the dark world of my remembrance.

I was standing in the kitchen of the old Victorian. I could make out a large refrigerator, stove, and microwave laced between newly hung maple cabinets with granite tops. If I was remembering standing in an old Victorian, it wasn't in the year 1900. My surroundings stood proof of that.

Just then a shot of pain jabbed into me. The shock broke my train of thought, derailing me back to do an inventory of my body. The source of the pain originated in my head. My skull felt like it was exploding from the inside out.

Dear God, please help me. Make this pain stop. My prayer surprised me. It felt more like I was imitating someone. Praying felt like a new experience to me. Maybe it was the feeling of the awful pain or maybe it was the feelings I had for the person who taught me to pray.

My first foray into prayer seemed to be working. My pain lessened to a point that I could return my thoughts back to exploring my memories of the old Victorian house.

Someone else shared the darkened interior with me, someone I wished to avoid. This person—no wait, these people were uninvited into the house. I felt no fear, only rage, as I raced through the floors of the old Victorian in an effort to avoid them. I knew every inch of the house and planned to use the darkness as an ally. I stealthily moved in the blackness, putting silent distance between the intruders and me. I felt almost victorious when I ran into an intruder face to face.

He appeared out of the shadowy darkness dressed in black, cloaking his position. I pushed at him and turned to run, veering in another direction. He hit me from behind. The blow was forceful and menacing. Shocking pain dropped me to my knees, but I knew I must keep moving. I staggered, half crawling in the darkness until I was standing on my feet again.

The throbbing pain I was experiencing now made sense. I had been fleeing from these intruders just before I leapt. The blow had stopped me temporarily and gave me a reason as to why I was having so much difficulty remembering what had happened to me.

I returned my focus back to the pounding in my head. I wanted to call for help or mercy, but my mouth was dry and my throat burned. It was difficult to swallow. My throat felt raw, but it didn't burn from screaming. I knew I was strong enough to face any danger. My throat hurt like I had been... strangled.

A flash of memory flickered in my parched head. I staggered to my feet after the skull-splitting blow and turned to confront my attacker. My fist made contact with his face, but instead of him falling backward, he lunged forward, grabbing my neck in both of his hands. His deadly grip restricted my breathing and forced the blood-pounding pain in my head to surge. I made two fists and brought my arms up between his. With a forceful spreading of my arms, I broke free of his chokehold. A half turn on my part and a side kick sent him hurtling down the staircase and into a lightless void.

I took a deep breath. Filling my lungs was difficult, restricted. I took another breath to expand my chest and could feel the binding of bandages wrapping me from below my arms to my waist. Another deep breath made the bandages tighten and pull against my back. A flash of searing pain forced another memory to surface.

I was familiar with the oblique bowels of the old Victorian house. I could feel my planned ascent to the top floor of the house. If I could reach the top floor, I was confident I would have enough time to escape being captured and leap without interference. I had taken out one of my assailants, but two more remained.

The eyes of my mind saw a door in front of me. I turned the knob and pushed my way in, turning to lock the door behind me, hoping to buy more time to leap, but the two intruders burst in. They flew silently at me like owls attacking their prey—o, not owls... falcons. My intruders were falcons, and they were out to capture or kill me at any cost.

I defended myself successfully, putting a room of distance between us. I grabbed at my crystal and readied myself to leap. I could feel my drift begin when a falcon caught me from behind. I squeezed my crystal tightly and concentrated on my leap, but my body was being pulled in two different directions. The flesh from my back was being torn off me by the falcon's firm hold.

I remembered my leap in clear definition now. Ally had leapt just moments before me, and I could still feel my desperation and need to follow her.

I inched my finger over the cool cotton I laid on. I was not lying on a bed but more of a cot, and she was not beside me.

I took a deep breath, expecting the sweet, comforting aroma of her lavender, but the smell of antiseptic and blood greeted me instead. I was in a hospital.

I strained my ears to hear through the white noise around me. I could make out the distant conversation of two women, but their voices were not familiar. They were discussing the care of another patient.

I knew I had to get to my feet and begin my search for Ally, but my strength and determination were held in check. I was sedated. It may have been the mounting pain or the sudden feeling of being alone, but I let the sedative pulsating in my veins win and drifted into sleep.

Chapter 21
Asylum

I awoke to bright sunlight glaring in my face. I blinked my eyes in an attempt to focus on my surroundings. The sharp sting of antiseptic still hung in the air. White, incoherent noise rang in my ears as the sunlight blinded me with its intensity.

I pulled myself to a sitting position and searched for the source of each individual piece of the white blanket of noise.

The room or ward I was confined to appeared to be more of an asylum than a hospital. The walls were a pallid white and badly in need of repainting. The windows on the wall opposite my cot were either dirty or painted over with the same bland white of the walls. I could make out a fine, interlocking mesh embedded in the glass. Bars also ran the length of each window, prohibiting any hope of escape.

The floors were made of cold grey concrete, which only added to the bleak, prison-like atmosphere. There were ten or fifteen cots along the wall facing me, mirroring the cots on my side of the room. The cots reached to each other like fingers stretching to intertwine, leaving just enough room for medical personal to walk the length of the room.

There were no curtains or drapes on either the windows or between the cots to afford the occupants any privacy.

I next looked at the faces of my fellow cellmates. The men who occupied the cots were suffering from various injuries. Some had limbs amputated, others had eyes blindingly bandaged shut, still others lay there lifeless. The worst of the lot thrashed in a frantic manner and moaned out incoherent mutterings. These men were tied to their beds with restraints. I was truly in an asylum. But why? What was wrong with me and why was I here?

I remembered the last moments of my leap more clearly now. I could see Ally's face, tear stained, as I pushed her into Tom's waiting arms. I could still here the sound of her voice pleading with me not to let her go. And I could feel the cold, empty void in my heart left in the wake of her leap. I had to find her. But how? I didn't even know where I was or when I was.

The locked doors at the end of the room clicked open, and two nurses dressed in white entered the ward. *I must be somewhere in time around World War II, judging by the white nurses uniforms and the military wounds my fellow roommates suffered*, I thought.

They pushed a cart of food-filled trays in front of them, stopping at each bed, placing a tray on the waiting patient's lap. Some men struggled to feed themselves, while others lay lifeless, staring at the ceiling, taking no notice of the food.

The two nurses offered no help but just made their rounds passing out the trays. As they came closer to me, I knew I had to take my chance and ask my questions quickly.

One nurse with brown, tied-back hair walked toward me carrying my breakfast. She was no more than thirty but looked much older from a distance. I could only contribute her haggard appearance to the stress of her occupation. She easily made eye contact with me as she approached.

"Good morning, John. It's nice to see you are awake. You have been with us for nearly three days. I was beginning to wonder if we should not have called you Sleeping Beauty instead of John."

She placed the tray on my lap and turned to leave. I reached out and touched her arm. She turned to me in response.

"What is it, John? Do you need something?"

John? Why was she calling me John? My name was David, and it never changed just because I leapt to a different time.

"Wha… Wha… d…d…day?"

"Good day to you too, John," she replied, misunderstanding my stuttering. "Dr. Johnston will be making the rounds soon. Now eat your breakfast and try to rest."

She turned, dismissing my needs, and proceeded to pass out the remaining food trays.

I tried to call after her. "Wh…wh…wh…" *Oh my God, I can't speak. What happened to me?* Did the blow to my head or the strangling I suffered leave me disabled? I was a prisoner of an asylum with no way to communicate with my keepers. *Oh dear God, what kind of hell am I in?*

I turned my attention to my breakfast as the hope of escape drained out of me. There was a small bowl of cold oatmeal and one cup of black coffee. My stomach burned from lack of food, so I ate and drank all that was put in front of me. The meager offering did little to stifle my hunger and more to accelerate the feeling of nausea it left in its wake.

The nurses returned to collect the trays, silently walking bed to bed. I held out the tray to the same nurse who had given it to me earlier.

"I told Dr. Johnston you were awake. He said to check your bandages and get you dressed. He wants to see you. I'll be back as soon as I finish picking up the breakfast trays." She smiled, flitting off to the next bed like a butterfly moving between flowers.

Maybe this Dr. Johnston will have some answers to the questions rushing like tides in and out of my head.

I looked around for any belongings I might have. All I wore was a back-less hospital gown with a sheet covering the bottom half of my body. I stretched to open the drawers of a metal cabinet next to my cot. Pulling open the top, I found it empty. No personal items. No crystal. I knew I had to be wearing my Saltanium crystal in order to leap, but it wasn't with me now. My panic grew. It was then my nurse returned.

"Okay, let's first get this gown off of you and change these bandages." She stripped me of my clothes as if undressing some mannequin. "Can you lay on your stomach for me?"

I complied. I could feel the cold steel of a scissor against my skin as she cut the binding from me. A blast of cold air blew over my back once it was exposed. The cold made the wounds sting all the more. She then washed the wounds with warm water and applied some type of an ointment.

"There. You are healing nicely. You should be able to move to a different ward in a few days. Could you please turn and sit up for me?"

I did as commanded.

"Hold your arms out so I can replace your bandages."

I stretched out my arms and she began to unwind a roll of white gauze, mummifying my back and chest again. When she was finished, she handed me some folded clothes and said, "Here, put these on. I'll be back in a few minutes to take you to Dr. Johnston."

I quickly pulled on a pair of white drawstring pants. They were too short for my frame, stopping mid calf. I put my arms in the sleeves of the oversized jacket and buttoned the only three buttons down the front before my Florence Nightingale returned.

"Can you stand and walk on your own, or do you need help?"

I slid myself off the bed and stood on a cold cement floor with my bare feet.

"Okay, let's go. Dr. Johnston is waiting," she said, pushing me to the locked doors of the ward.

Chapter 22

Parade

The nurse escorted me out of the ward and down a long hallway. The corridor was lined with doors I could only assume concealed more wards full of injured men. A large, black, walnut door with a frosted-glass window stood sentry at the end of the hallway. The nurse knocked on the glass, opened it, and directed me to follow her in.

The room seemed devoid of color, like it had been torn from an old black-and-white movie. A massive desk, also made of black walnut, ate most of the space in the room. A glass window, frosted and barred, stood behind the desk, and two worn leather chairs stood in front. The chairs' leather covering seemed to be the exact same shade of dull brown as everything else in the room.

An exhausted-looking, bald, middle-aged man sat behind the desk. I could only assume him to be the Dr. Johnston the nurse spoke of.

The nurse began the introduction. "Good morning, Dr. Johnston. This is the patient you asked about from ward five. You said you wanted to speak to him once he was up, so here he is."

"John, this is Dr. Johnston." The nurse then handed a file envelope to the doctor and left.

Dr. Johnston stood up from behind the desk separating us and reached out to shake my hand. "Hello, I'm Dr. Johnston. Won't you have a sit, John?" His accent was somewhere between Irish and English.

I sat in a chair opposite the desk, as directed.

"Can you remember anything about where you were or how you got here?"

I shook my head no. I did remember what happened to me just before I leapt, but I knew relaying that story would confirm any opinion on the doctor's part that I was insane. I had to be free of this hospital if I ever was to begin looking for Allyson.

"Wh… where… am… I?"

"You are in a military hospital just outside of London, in Canterbury. You were found on a road in Northern France about two weeks ago. Your clothes looked like they had been shredded; but based on the color, it was assumed you were part of the Allied Forces, so you were brought here."

He then began reading my file. "You suffered a severe blow to the head, and your back gives every indication you were also tortured. Do you remember anything before waking up here?"

Again I shook my head no. I made the sign of writing in the air in hopes of being supplied with a better way to communicate my questions, but the doctor ignored my request.

Dr. Johnston opened the side drawer of his desk and took out a manila envelope marked "John Doe, 13."

"This is all you had with you. We found no dog tags to tell us who you are, but you were wearing some remnants of an American uniform."

He spilled the contents of the envelope onto his desk. My heart pounded at the sight of my crystal of Saltanium. I reached to pick it up.

"Do you remember you name or your family?"

"I… cannot… s…speak. Why?"

"We expect your speech to return to normal eventually, but it will take some therapy. Your brain suffered a trauma similar to a stroke."

I made a movement again indicating I would like to write. This time the doctor gave me a pad of paper and a pencil.

I cannot remember my name or how I got here, but I do feel I have family or someone special waiting for me. When can I leave?

"You can't leave until you are more recovered. Besides, I cannot release you if you are suffering from amnesia. As far as your family goes, I have received several letters from families searching for lost loved ones. I will write to them and see if any of them remember you."

I couldn't see how Allyson could possibly find me. She leapt while we were in America, so she should still be there. I ended up in Europe probably due to the Falcon pulling me back during my leap. I would have to find Ally. She could never find me.

What if no one can be found?

"I think you will be well enough to leave in a month or so. Right now, I'll have a nurse take you to your new room and get you some clothes that fit you better. I'll check on you tomorrow to see how you are doing."

He rang a silent bell and an orderly entered to escort me to my new room.

We walked down a different corridor also lined with locked doors. The room we entered was about one-third of the size of the ward I woke up in. It smelled musty and dirty, most likely due to the discarded, used pieces of furniture in the space. There were five cots lining the walls, a small card table in the center, and one large tattered couch. The only light in the space was provided by a single light bulb dangling from the ceiling. There were no windows in the room, making it feel more like a large closet than a hospital ward.

Four men in military uniforms were playing a game of cards at the table, and the orderly introduced me to my new roommates.

"Gentlemen, you have a new roommate. This is John. John this is Charlie, Jason, Bill, and another John Doe."

Charlie wore dark glasses. I could tell he had impaired vision by the way he tilted his head to read the cards he held. Jason sat in a chair, catatonic, staring out at nothing. The other John Doe stared back at me with lifeless eyes. Only Bill acknowledged my entrance.

"Hello, mate. So you are the other John Doe they said to expect." Bill had the same Irish/English accent as the doctor. "Well, best of luck to you," he said as he patted me on my back.

I still had the pad of paper and pencil the doctor had given me, so I wrote: *How can I get out of here?*

"Oh, great, you can't speak. I was hoping to have someone to talk to. Well, mate, the only way out of here is the parade."

Parade?

"Yes. You see, unless someone comes for you or they are able to identify who you are, you stay here. The never-ending array of all the broken-hearted hopefuls looking for their lost loved ones, that is the parade. The doc basically puts you on display. At best, someone will recognize you, and you will go home. At worst, you'll watch as the mothers, fathers, wives, sisters, brothers, aunts, uncles—it doesn't matter if you are not the person they are looking for—get their hearts ripped out and their hopes drained from them. You better pray you have a family that is willing to look for you and they find you quickly."

The hope of being with Ally again was being drained out of me like my life's blood. I had no idea where Ally was or even if she had leapt into 1940. The reality of my situation caused panic to sear through every cell in my body.

Weeks passed. I sat day after day in my prison. Occasionally I was called to meet somebody looking for their son, husband, brother, nephew, but I knew it was never me they looked for. When I wasn't on display or in speech therapy, I sat by myself. Occasionally I played cards with my other roommates, poker mostly, betting with matchsticks. The only book to read was the Bible.

Reading the Bible gave me hope, hope that someday I would be freed and I would find Ally. But it was difficult to maintain a positive outlook while the days passed and distance between us grew.

I had read nearly half the Bible and was now on Psalms when I came across Psalm 39:

I was mute with silence... and my sorrow was stirred up... Hear my prayer, O Lord... regain my strength, before I go away and am no more.

Regain my strength before I am no more became my new mantra. I recited it over and over again. God put Ally and me together, and I believed He would not keep us apart. I prayed my mantra, knowing without Ally I would be "no more." I couldn't exist without her.

Chapter 23

Station

Monotony became my daily routine. Time felt better measured with a calendar than a watch. Weeks grew into months. Every day was identical to the day before: three tasteless meals of paste-like cereal, watery soup, stale bread, and disgusting coffee. I killed time like it was killing me by playing poker sporadically with my fellow inmates or reading the Bible, and, yes, there was the occasional interruption of the "parade." Every other day, one or more of us were summoned to Dr. Johnston's office to be displayed to some hopeful family looking for their loved one. But my excursions to the parade always ended the same: No one came for me.

I planned on leaping as soon as I could get my hands on my Saltanium, but Dr. Johnston kept it locked up tightly, almost as tightly as he did me.

The days left me numb and drained, but the nights were my true torture, especially the nights it rained. I could hear the tapping of each raindrop as it splattered against the oblique glass of the window. I would lie there and let myself be transported back to that glorious night Ally first slept in my arms, the night she was frightened by the storm. I could almost feel her breathe in and out in time with my heartbeats. But I would open my eyes to the reality that she was not here. I had no idea where she was, what was happening to her, or how I would ever find her again.

Sleeping became increasingly difficult. My mind burned with memories of us together. My body ached from her absence in my life. My heart beat out every second of our separation. Hope poured from me like blood from a deep, fatal wound. I was dying.

I sat up most nights reading, hoping to find a reprieve, but even the Bible pulled my thoughts back to Allyson. I had read up to the Song of Solomon. I felt a communion with him as I read his words, words describing the feelings I kept locked up.

> I sleep but my heart is awake. – My heart yearned for her – But my beloved was gone. – I sought her, but couldn't find her. I called but she gave no answer. – Where has my beloved gone, O fairest among women? – That I may seek you.

One evening, Bill returned from his spin on the parade, but this time he looked more alive.

"It's your turn, Johnny my boy. I don't know if this one is for you, but she is quite the looker. Take you time and enjoy the scenery," he said, slapping my back.

I followed the orderly to the same familiar door, knocked, and walked into the room. I had been in Dr. Johnston's office at night before, but this time the room seemed foreboding. The one gooseneck lamp stationed on his desk made a blinding cone of bright white in contrast to the blackness. As my eyes adjusted to the light, I could make out the shape of a young woman sitting in the armchair across from Dr. Johnston's desk. I must have finally lost my mind, because I stared at the back of her head finding comfort in the fact her hair was the same color as Ally's.

Just then Dr. Johnston turned the gooseneck lamp up so I was bathed in its cone of white, blinding light. I squinted against the sudden shock to my cornea.

"Is this the man you are looking for?" I heard him ask.

There was a moment of silence, and then the woman answered, "Yes, that's my husband. How soon can he be released?"

"Well, there are a few things you need to know about John first."

I couldn't believe my ears. Surely I must be dreaming. Was it Ally's voice I was hearing? I walked out of the light to see her face.

She continued her conversation with Dr. Johnston, oblivious to my movements. As her face came into view, I felt the blood rush from my head and my heart pound out of my chest. It was Ally.

I dropped to my knees at her feet and stared up at her, interrupting her conversation. "Do... kn... know.... M... me?"

"What's wrong with him, Doctor? Why is he speaking like that?"

"John suffered some head trauma during what we believe to be torture, but he has no memories of what happened to him or who he is. His bodily wounds have healed, leaving behind some pretty nasty scars, but he still has trouble speaking. John receives daily speech therapy. I can show you what you need to do to continue the therapy, if you like."

I continued to stare at her. Why was she ignoring me? Surely she recognized me. She called me her husband. I reached to touch her hand, but she pulled her hand back as if the touch of my fingers was acid on her skin. She looked at me with contemptuous eyes, briefly and swiftly turning her attention back to the doctor.

The doctor continued to speak. "Other than a few papers you need to sign, you can take John home with you tonight."

"John? Why do you call him John?"

She knew my name wasn't John. Hope began to grow.

The doctor answered, "We call all our patients who are suffering from amnesia John Doe. Hopefully, with your help, his memories can be restored, or relearned at least."

I touched Ally's hand again to get her attention and also to convince myself that she was not a mirage. "M… my… n… name," I said, pointing to myself.

She recoiled from my touch again. Staring back coldly, she answered, "James… Your name is James Stevens."

With that said, she turned her attention back to the doctor, ignoring me.

Something was terribly wrong. Why didn't she say my name was David? After all, she did tell the doctor I was her husband. Who was James Stevens?

The doctor interrupted my thoughts. "John—I'm sorry, James, why don't you go back to your room and pack your things? I'll finish briefing your wife. Meet us back here. You can leave as soon as the paperwork is completed."

I left as directed and walked back to my room in a stupor. A mix of emotions filled me. First, my prayers were answered. Allyson had found me, and we were together again. But she didn't know me, and I couldn't image why.

Bill greeted me as soon as I walked into the room. "Well, John, how did it go? Wasn't she a lot better to look at than some of the old long, sad faces we usually see?"

I nodded yes and started to pack the few belongings I had in the room.

"Oh, no! She is here for you? Who is she, you lucky dog?"

I wrote "my wife" on a pad of paper and handed it to Bill.

"Well, you are one lucky bastard. Not only do you get to leave this hellhole, you can bed a beauty tonight."

I ignored Bill's remark. Hearing him speak about Ally as someone to bed made me furious. I quickly made the rounds, shaking hands good-bye, happy to finally be leaving. Then I grabbed my bag, swung it over my shoulder, and walked from the room to return to Ally.

Dr. Johnston had just completed his instructions and was handing Ally the manila envelope containing my personal effects. She folded it into her bag without opening it and shook Dr. Johnston hands. I stuttered out "thank you" and followed Ally out of the hospital.

We entered a waiting taxi waiting outside. The cold, moist blast of night air refreshed me. I held the door of the taxi open, and Ally got in. I stepped in after her, sharing the back seat. We were alone and, for the first time in a millennium, together; but she still remained cold, silent, and distant from me.

She instructed the cabbie to take us to the Canterbury Station and turned to watch out the window as if no one was with her. We rode in silence. She made no attempt to speak or acknowledge my presence. I, on the other hand, had to fight every desire within me not to touch her. I had Ally back, but she wasn't my Ally.

The train station was deserted when we arrived. She walked directly to the clerk, checked the schedule, and then returned to me.

"Our train doesn't leave until morning. We just have to sit and wait." She finished her curt statement without making any eye contact and sat down on the closest wooden bench.

I sat down beside her to wait out the remainder of the night. I tried to think of reasons why she had not checked us into a hotel until morning. Maybe she lacked the money to pay for it, but she look very well off, so I dismissed that theory. Maybe she was afraid we would somehow miss our train, but we could walk from any hotel in the area to the train station in less than an hour. Or maybe, just maybe, she was afraid to be alone with me.

We sat like two statues staring forward, ignoring each other. She moved to the end of the bench, increasing the space between us. The only sound in the station was the ticking of the large clock hung on the wall as it measured out the hours.

I closed my eyes, but I knew I wouldn't sleep. Then I felt her head lean against my shoulder. I looked down at her to find her in a deep sleep. *Her body must have rested against mine involuntarily* I thought. I decided to take advantage of this wonderful happenstance. I put my bag in my lap and moved my arm so she would slide down my body and into my lap. I reached to pull her legs up on to the seat of the bench and covered her with my coat. She stirred only once to nestle more deeply against my body.

I looked down at the sleeping Ally of my remembrance. This Ally had the same hair color as my Ally. Of course, my Ally wore her hair braided into a long rope running down her back; this Ally wore her hair tied back loosely into a bun.

I brushed a stray hair from her face lightly with my fingers, and she sighed in response to my touch. Oh God, I wanted to bend down, lift her face to mine, and kiss her. But I dared not move for fear I would wake her and suffer rejection. This new Ally didn't want to have any contact with me, and she made that very clear. She may not want me, but I needed her, so I was content to take advantage of this tender moment and let her sleep in my lap.

I continued my inventory of my wife. Small golden loops laced through her soft, pierced lobes. My Ally didn't have pierced ears because she said needles made her ill. I lightly traced the outline of her ear, but I would rather have nibbled at them like I used to do.

I breathed in her scent. She was washed in a mixture of lavender with a slight mingling of vanilla. I thought heaven must have lavender lining the halls because that was my Ally's aroma. The hint of vanilla only intensified my yearning, making me hungrier for the taste of her skin.

I wanted to at least kiss her cheek, but I resigned myself to lightly stroking her hair and passing the night. She slept peacefully in my lap. I could have slept also, but I didn't want to miss a moment of having her close to me again. I knew that this Ally, unlike my Ally, would not yearn for my touch once she woke.

Chapter 24

Ship

I must have fallen asleep because I opened my eyes to the grey light of morning filtering into the depot, producing a monotone world I was accustomed to. I looked down at the angel in my lap to make sure Ally was still real and I wasn't dreaming.

She was still sleeping peacefully, fitted against me so perfectly she seemed an extension of me. I lightly traced the contours of her hair, and she sighed, turning to nestle her face into my stomach. I held my muscles tightly so as not to disturb her, but it also helped me to control the passion I felt building inside of me.

She took a deep breath in and blinked her eyes opened. For a moment, we stared at each other, partners in the same dream. Her eyes, her beautiful aqua-green eyes—I realized that was the color I missed the most when I was trapped in my black-and-white prison. Her eyes were the color of a cool lake on a summer's day. And the water in the pool of her eyes spilled over and poured into me, restoring like rain on a desert.

And then, she jumped to her feet, throwing my coat to the floor, and glared at me with disgust. The spring of aqua green had frozen into an unrecognizable ice lake.

I hoped *this* Ally's reaction might be caused by the propriety of 1940: no public displays of affection. I feared she really was disgusted by my close proximity. I stammered out, "No... m... mar...married," wishing to quell any embarrassment she felt and hoping my first theory was correct.

"We are not *that* kind of married," she returned coldly. She quickly gathered her belongings, produced our tickets, and instructed me, "Get your things. I'm sure we can board the train by now." She led the way, and I followed her past the clerk, conductor, and finally into our cabin of the train.

"You sit on that side," she said pointing. "I'll sit over here."

Again we sat in silence, she staring out the window and me staring at her. I wanted to make use of our time together by talking to her, but my stammering only made me sound like some kind of a demented fool. I dug in my pocket for the pad of paper and pen I carried to every session with Dr. Johnston and wrote:

My name is James Stevens. What is your name?

She looked down at the paper and said, "Abigail Stevens."

How long have we been married?

"About three years."

How did we meet?

"My father had a small but successful business, and you fancied yourself a great entrepreneur. You *had* to have my father's company so, when he refused to sell it, you *married* me to get it."

We didn't marry out of love?

She laughed a raw, bitter cackle. "Yes, we married for love. I loved you. You loved winning."

So I never loved you?

"I don't think you are capable of loving anyone but yourself."

It was obvious the marriage of James and Abigail Stevens was nothing like the marriage Ally and I shared. I loved her beyond all imagining. If my Ally was locked up somewhere inside Abigail, I would have to get past all the damage James had left first.

The train finally pulled out of the station. We chugged along the English landscape in silence. Abigail was content to avoid me.

I used the time to make sense of what was happening with this leap. Ally, or Abigail, had come looking for me, but what had happened in the leap to make her forget me? She looked, felt, and smelled like Ally, so why were we stuck in this James and Abby story? And my most maddening thought: How would I ever be able to get Ally back?

The train pulled into the station, and Abigail quickly picked up her things and rushed off the train with no regard for me. I scrambled to follow and finally caught sight of her on the platform. She was scanning the station as if looking for someone.

"Alec," she shouted, waving her hand above her hand and running through the crowd.

Wading through the crowd was like walking in quicksand, but I had to catch up with her before I lost her again. I saw her rush into someone's arms. The tall man folded her against him, opening his long tan coat to invite her in.

We recognized each other even at a distance. It was Tom, my *dear* brother. He held her tightly against him and looked up, making eye contact with me. Once he had my audience, he lifted her face to his and kissed her. I could feel the urge to rip him from her burning in me, but I held my emotions in check for fear an outburst would only frighten Abigail away.

She pulled away from his kiss like she pulled away from me in the station. I happily noted Abigail didn't like Tom's advances any more than I like watching them.

I continued to stare at Tom even as I grew close and joined the pair. I could tell he knew exactly who I was.

"I'm so glad you are back with me safe and sound. Is this him?" he said as we still stood locked in each other's vision.

"Yes, this is James. I found him at the hospital where the doctor had answered my letter. He is suffering from some physical injuries, and, according to the doctor, he has amnesia. Oh, there is also something wrong with his speech, but therapy should restore it."

He turned his eyes from me to look at Abigail. "Well, he doesn't have to remember you or say a word to give you a divorce. He just has to be able to sign the papers."

Looking up to make sure I still had my eyes locked on him, Tom continued, "Where did you two sleep last night?"

"I did just as you instructed. We didn't stay at a hotel but sat up all night in the train station."

"You must be exhausted. You can rest once we board the boat to America."

"Actually, I did sleep a little at the station." She quickly glanced at me to make sure I wasn't going to give her away by saying she slept in my lap.

The three of us then squeezed into the back seat of a waiting taxi. Tom—or Alec, as she called him—and I sat by the doors. Abigail sat between us, but she leaned into Tom's arm and he pulled her closer to him. I could feel the rage and jealousy returning. I had trusted him to take care of her. I put her into his arms to allow her to leap safely, and now he was using that trust to take her from me.

Arriving at the dock, we were greeted by a titanic ocean liner. We walked up the gangplank to the main deck. Once on board I could see the ship was more a maritime vessel than an ocean liner. The stark deck was filled with people, mostly military personal, and there were very few amenities.

"I reserved two rooms for us if you would like to get some rest." I could see how it was going to be. Tom, or Alec, and Abigail would talk to each other as if I didn't exist.

"Two? What did you think we were going to do with *two* rooms?" Abigail's tone surprised me. She was truly upset with Alec, and I was enjoying her rage.

"I thought that you and I…" Alec began sheepishly.

"I am not sharing a room with him or you. What kind of a woman do you think I am? You may be the only man in my life right now, but I will not be scandalized by your assumptions. I will not share a cabin with you, and I'm definitely not sharing one with him. I'll take the smaller cabin, and you two can share the other one."

Alec dropped a key into her waiting hand, and she stormed off to find her room, leaving Alec and I to face each other.

"Shall we find our room then?" Alec didn't wait for me to answer but led the way.

Upon reaching the room, he opened the door and we walked in. I shut the door and turned to him and said, "Wh... what... are... you... d... doing... with... m... my... wife?"

"Oh no! This is too good to be true. You really can't speak."

I pulled out my pad of paper and pen and wrote:

My speech may be impaired, but I remember everything that happened before the leap. You promised to take care of her not take her for yourself.

"You know it is just too easy competing against a boy like you," he said, laughing. "Yes, I wanted her for myself, but how to get her away from you? The answer was really so easy. You fell for my excuse about letting her leap with me because she would be safer. You really are naïve. Did you ever stop to think we could have switched crystals and you could have leapt with her? You would be with her right now; but no, you passed her into my waiting arms."

I am with her now.

"No, she doesn't remember you at all. You see, my crystal is able to carry two people. One is the falcon, and other is the spore. I'll speak slowly so you can try to understand. Spores only have to be captured once. Do you know why? I'll tell you. Spores only have to be captured once because the leap erases their memory."

He waited for me to respond, but I just glared back at him, containing my desire to strangle him.

"No, you still don't get it, do you? You see, it wouldn't matter if she leapt with you or me. A leap with you on one crystal would surely have killed her, and a leap with me on a falcon crystal was guaranteed to erase any trace of her existence before the leap. I knew my chances of winning her heart would be better if she couldn't remember you. I just couldn't believe you actually were stupid enough to let me take her with me. She woke up on the other side of the leap with no memory of you and in *my* arms. So, you see, I win."

Why did she come for me then? Maybe Ally does remember me, it is just hidden deep within her.

"Do you know anything about the woman you call your wife? Don't answer. It's a rhetorical question. I can see you don't. Let me explain. Your wife is a Halo. Halos don't leap like you and I. They are genetically bound when they leap. Ally has leapt into her great grandmother, Abigail Stevens. Her great grandmother was searching for her husband. Ally wasn't searching for you, Abigail was searching for James."

But I'm still her husband.

"Not for long. Abigail is filing for divorce as soon as we dock, and then it is so long to you."

You are wrong. She will remember me. I know I can make her love me again.

"One more time, your wife is in her great grandmother's body. She has to give birth to Ally's grandmother, who has her mother, who has Ally. You can't stop that without changing history."

I'm not stupid. I know that.

"Do you know what Ally's grandmother's maiden name was?"

I shook my head no.

"Denby. Her grandmother's name was Melissa Denby."

So what?

"Your name is Stevens. I am Alec Denby. If Abigail doesn't have a child with me, the Ally you knew will be erased completely. Do you understand now? Unless Abigail marries me and leaves you behind, your precious Ally will never be born. You see, brother, I win any way you look at it."

Alec slithered from the room like the snake he was. I knew there had to be a way to get Ally to remember me. I made up my mind to try everything in my power to win her back regardless of his theory.

Chapter 25

Agreement

Abigail was almost a shadow to every movement Alec made. She never strayed more than a few feet from his side. He, not I, was the safe harbor she searched for.

We ate our meals in a large dining room shared with the other passengers aboard the ship. Our table was barely able to seat two people let alone three. Abigail and Alec ate their dinner close together while engaging in polite conversation, both totally ignoring my presence.

I took my imposed invisibility as an opportunity to observe every nuisance of Abigail's behavior. I searched for flickers of the Ally I knew and loved sparkling though Abigail's cold veneer. I knew I could never get enough of her, regardless of how she felt for me.

I could tell by the way she acted with Alec she regarded him as just a friend and not a lover. I knew what passion looked like on her, and, to my relief, she didn't exhibit that glow toward him.. She seemed to lean on him more as a protector. This gave me hope I might be able to make her fall back in love with me, but any hope I had burning inside me was always squelched when I made contact with her. Her reaction to the slightest touch was always the same: shock, fear, and recoiling. I knew James must have done something terrible to her to create this lack of trust. I had to find out what happened between them if I was ever going to overcome her feelings for James.

It was easy to disappear undetected after dinner and return to the cabin I shared with Alec. I laid in my bed thinking of ways I might break through to Abigail to reach Ally. I had to believe Ally still existed somewhere deeply hidden inside Abigail. I reasoned getting her to relive moments of our life together, like the night of the thunderstorm, our first kiss, or our honeymoon, perhaps then her memory would be jarred. But every plan I had would require me touching her, and Abigail was repulsed by James in every way.

The evening passed into night. Sleep eluded me just like it had every night since I landed in 1940. I knew it was because I lacked the most important part of my tranquility: Ally. My yearning for her now was only increased knowing she slept just a few feet from me. So close, yet so far from my touch.

Abigail planned on leaving me as soon as we docked. I had less than thirty-six hours left at my disposal to convince her to stay. If I could get her to agree to postpone the divorce and stay with me until the end of the year, I might be able to reach Ally.

I sat up in bed and turned on the small light next to me. I took out my pad of paper and pen and started drafting a letter of agreement requesting Abigail stay with me after we docked to help with my speech therapy and memory recovery. I wrote down a daily schedule of therapy times and time for Abigail to answer my questions about James. Holding the divorce papers Abigail wanted so badly as ransom might buy me enough time to convince her to stay with me. I knew I could never let her go.

I feverishly wrote down all the aspects of my plan while listening to the sounds of Alec sleeping. He slept uninterrupted with the confidence of a man who felt certain of victory, a victory that would win him my Ally. But it was a victory I could not and would not let him have.

When I finished I returned to lying sleepless in my bed. Morning came. Alec woke and left the cabin without a word. It was obvious he had no need of me.

I left the cabin shortly after and followed him to the upper deck. As I walked up the stairway I could see him talking to Abigail. He was sitting on a deck chair facing her, and she was lying on her stomach on one of the wooden lounges next to him. Her face was covered by a large picture hat shielding her face from the sun.

I stopped close enough to hear and observe them without being detected. "Are you sure I can't get you any breakfast?" Alec asked.

"I'm positive. This headache is making me nauseous. I think I will just lay here in the sun. It feels good on my back. You go ahead and get something to eat. I'll be here when you get back."

Alec walked away from her and toward the galley.

I took this as my chance to be alone with her. I walked up and sat down on the chair vacated by Alec. Abigail must have thought I was Alec. She said, "You're back so soon? Did you change your mind about getting something to eat?"

I decided to take advantage of her assumption, so I hummed at a yes.

She continued talking. "I couldn't sleep again last night. I don't know why I can't sleep. It's driving me crazy. It has been almost two months of insomnia. I guess I'll have to make an appointment to see a doctor once we get home. I just don't like the idea of taking medication to sleep, but I'm desperate."

Two months—the amount of time since our leap. She couldn't sleep just like me because my Ally needed me as must as I needed her. There was hope I could get Ally to remember me. Her body was involuntarily on my side.

She moved, twisting in an effort to relax the muscles in her back.

I seized the opportunity to touch her. I began to message her neck and shoulders, working my hands down her spine to the small of her back. She sighed under my touch, and her muscles softened and relaxed. I took a deep breath and let my heart pound with growing desire.

"Mmm, that is heaven. I wish you could have done this last night. Maybe I could have slept a little."

"What have we here?" Alec boomed, interrupting our tender moment.

Ally looked out from under the hat to see Alec standing behind me. She stood quickly, pulling away from my hands and taking her usual place clinging to Alec's arm. Half hidden behind him, she stared at me with those all too familiar frightened eyes.

"Get me out of here," she begged Alec, and they left.

I stayed clear of her the rest of the day and worked on my plan. I included my need for two daily speech therapies. She would have to agree to do therapy with me as per Dr. Johnston's instruction. Secondly, she needed to fill me in on my missing memories, or James's missing memories. This should give me at least a month or two to soften her fear of James and find out more of what transpired between them during their marriage.

When I finished to my satisfaction, I folded the perfected agreement and placed it in my pocket. Now all I had to do was find a way to give it to her without involving Alec.

Alec made sure to keep Abigail from me for the remainder of the second day aboard the ship. I took his actions as a personal victory. He wouldn't guard her so fiercely if he didn't perceive me as some kind of a threat.

At midnight I was still not able to sleep and left the cabin for a walk on deck. It was as I walked up the stairway to the main deck I noticed her.

She stood washed in moonlight looking like an angel too heavenly to be of this earth.

I walked slowly toward her. "A…" I stopped myself. I couldn't call her Ally. "A… Abby."

She turned to the sound of my voice. "Oh it's you. Did you just call me Abby?"

I nodded yes.

"You never call me Abby. It's always Abigail. I think it was just your way of being cold and distant, no pet names."

"S… s… s…orry."

"No, it's okay. I kind of like being called Abby, Jimmy."

I smiled. This was the most relaxed she had ever been around me. Confident she wouldn't vanish, I handed her the paper mapping out the arrangement.

"What's this?"

"A... rr... ange...ment"

"Arrangement?" She opened the paper and read it. "You want me to stay with you until the end of the year to help with your therapy and memory?"

I nodded yes.

"It says here you will sign the divorce papers, letting me go, one way or the other, at the end of the year. You would really do that, sign the divorce papers, no questions asked, and let me go?"

"Yes."

"You have changed. The James I knew would never be this considerate. I guess I could stay for awhile, but I would have to tell Alec and get his approval first."

She was back gasping for Alec.

I wanted to keep her in the moment, so I asked, "Can... not.... s... s...leep?"

"No, I can't sleep. You know, it's funny, the last time I slept was in the train station with you."

I sat down on a deck chair and opened my arms to her. "Sleep... now."

She almost took a step toward me but stopped, saying, "I can't. How would it look?"

"Bad... to... Alec?"

"Oh, I don't care what he thinks."

"You... sleep... with... him?"

"No! I refuse to break a commandment. Besides, we are just friends."

"But... d...divorce."

"That is your fault, not mine. I would be happy to stay with you if you gave me a family, but as I said, we don't have *that* kind of a marriage. Divorce is my only hope. Maybe I could find someone someday who would like to have a family with me."

I opened my arms again and gestured for her to come to me.

"I can't. I just don't trust you." She took a step closer and continued, "There is a piece of me that knows you will hurt me again, but there is another piece that remembers sleeping with you at the station and the unsolicited back rub this morning. I never felt so relaxed. It was like I found a piece of me that was missing."

"Trust... me. Now... sleep... here." I opened my arms to her, but this time she moved to sit next to me.

"I want you to know that I still don't trust you. I'm only going to take you up on this offer because I have to get some sleep before I go crazy. But you have to promise me you won't take advantage of me... or hurt me."

"P...p...romise."

She sighed deeply and laid down on the chaise next to mine.

I took the blanket from the back of my chaise, opened it, and wrapped it around me and laid down next to her. In one fluid move I scooped my arm under her, pulled her on top of me, and closed the blanket around us.

She gasped at the suddenness of my movement and pushed against my chest to create more distance between us. Her body stiffened and her breathing seemed panicked. What had James done to his wife to make her fear him so?

I rested my cheek on the top of her head and closed my eyes, content to have her in my arms again. I hoped that my stillness would calm her fears. I breathed in her familiar scent of lavender and vanilla.

She sighed again and began to relax. She moved, fitting her head against the contours of my chest as if to listen to my heart beating a lullaby, and then looked up at me. "Thank you," is all she said before returning her head to my chest, closing her eyes.

"You… well…come," I said and kissed the top of her head before we fell asleep.

Chapter 26

Home

I woke up alone on the windswept deck of the ship. The morning sky was grey and cold in typical fall fashion. Abigail must have left me sometime before dawn, not willing to risk Alec finding out how she spent the night. I deluded myself into thinking she felt some kind of an affection growing between us. Why else would she want to avoid bringing Alec into the picture?

I knew we docked today, so I returned to the cabin to ready myself. Alec was up and smugly packing his things. "You look like hell," was the greeting I received as I entered our room.

I quickly wrote down something and passed it to him.

I couldn't sleep. I went for a walk on deck and sat to watch the ocean and dozed off.

He laughed as he read it. Smug reassurance oozed from him like sweat.

I smiled back at him and let him enjoy his delusional victory. My silence held the secret that Abigail, or Ally, had been with me all night.

We joined Abigail in the galley for breakfast. She still clung to Alec but occasionally looked up to see if I was watching her. She never returned my smile and still recoiled from the touch of my hand, but she did, however, keep the secret of our encounter on deck the night before.

The ship docked, and we disembarked into a waiting taxi. We sat as before, Alec on one side and me on the other. Abigail sat between us, but this time she didn't lean against Alec. She sat erect, stiff backed, with her hands folded ladylike in her lap. She still wouldn't touch me, but the fact she wasn't touching him was a personal victory.

We drove along in the taxi in silence. Signs dotted the sided of the road announcing we were on our way to Somerset.

At first the landscape was unfamiliar—after all, it was 1940. All the land-marks I knew in 2000 would not even be constructed yet. I was not, however, prepared for what awaited me when the taxi stopped.

We stepped out and waited at the curb while the driver retrieved our bags from the trunk. I stared up at the old Victorian house majestically standing on the top of the walk. It was our house or, at least, the house we shared with Don and Samantha. I couldn't believe my eyes.

She must have seen the stunned look on my face. "Do you remember the house?" Abigail said, touching the sleeve of my coat to gain my attention.

I did not respond. Never in my wildest imaginings did I think the house Abigail shared with James would be the same house Don bought for Samantha. But there it stood, looking amazingly familiar. It was the same old, comfortable, inviting Victorian I met Ally in; the same house we were married in; the same house we first lived together in. It was the same house only somewhat newer since it was 1940, more than sixty years before she and I would live here. Surely I could use this setting to help Ally remember me and what we shared.

"Well, do you?" Ally's second question brought me back to reality.

"No," I replied, looking down at her and covering my emotions.

"Come inside, and I'll show you around," she said, tugging at my sleeve.

We entered the house, and, other than the 1940s interior, the house was remarkably the same. The entryway still greeted us with the same floor and ceiling light. The parlor had the same furniture arrangement but with the couch facing the radio instead of a flat-screen television. The walls were covered with an intricately patterned wallpaper, and the windows were blocked by heavy burgundy drapes; but other than that, the room was remarkably un-changed.

Abigail continued her pull on the sleeve of my coat as we toured the first floor. By now she had her arm wrapped around mine, so it was difficult to discern who was leading. I stopped at the fireplace and stood on the hearth. This was the same hearth we exchanged our vows on. I looked at Abigail, yearning to see some flash of memory, of Ally, but the aqua-green eyes looking back belonged to Abigail.

Abigail nudged me again, and we walked through to the formal dining room. I stopped again and stared at the chandelier. This was the same chan-delier we had our wedding dinner under. Again, Abigail seemed unaware.

We proceeded to the kitchen. It was odd to see a pull-chain ceiling light where track lighting should be. An oak table anchoring the center of the room stood instead of the island we ate at. The icebox, though, was in the same spot where the refrigerator would stand, the refrigerator I lifted Ally down from. I smiled when I looked at the spot on the linoleum floor and remembered Ally falling on top of me as we lost our balance. I could remember how much I wanted to kiss her at that moment, but this memory was mine alone. Abigail showed no reaction to our surroundings.

She proceeded on the tour, and I followed her back around and to the main staircase. She started up the stairs with me dutifully in tow. I hesitated on the balcony and turned to look down at the living room. A flash of memory soldered me in place. It was here I met Ally for the first time.

"Do you remember something?" she question again.

But just the fact she needed to ask made me realize Ally was deeply buried in Abigail, if she even existed at all.

I shook my head no and continued to follow her.

She walked to the top of the staircase, turned to face me, and said, "Do you remember your mother?"

"No." I didn't care if James remembered his mother. I wanted, needed, for Ally to remember me.

"You were very close to her, especially after your father died. This was her house. You grew up here. You brought me here to live after we were married. I'm sorry to tell you this, but your mother had a stroke when she received the letter stating you were missing. She died two months ago. Her death was the main reason I came for you. I promised her I would not give up looking for you until I found you. It was her last request, and I could never refuse her anything. She always treated me kindly, and sometimes I felt like she was my mother too."

She must have misconstrued by confusion for remorse. She continued, "I'm so very sorry. Please know your mother loved you very much. Your name was the last thing she said before she died."

"I hope you don't mind, but I took over your mother's room. I moved my things in here to take care of her after the stroke. I can move back into our room, and you can have this one, if you would feel more comfortable."

"No. You... st...stay." I looked around the room that would someday belong to Don and Samantha. The idea of a loving married couple sharing the room was in sharp contrast to the cold reality of my marriage to Abigail. Her words to me—"We are not that kind of married"— cut even deeper now.

We walked the second-floor promenade to the adjoining rooms Ally and I shared.

"This is your room," she said, opening the door.

I peered inside. The wall supporting the adjoining door was missing, and the two separate rooms we once shared were one large suite. I walked to the bed against the far wall and looked back at the window, letting a flash of memory flood over me. I could see Ally standing with the morning sunlight behind her. She had spent the night in my arms, in my bed, seeking refuge from a thunderstorm. I couldn't allow myself to act on the desire I had for her, so I ordered her to leave my bed. She walked, slowing as she got to her room and stopping in the doorway to thank me. I will never forget the sight of her. Every mouthwatering curve of her body was accentuated by the dawning light behind her. I could still feel the strength it took for me to not reach out and pull her back into my bed.

Abigail interrupted my latest excursion into the past. "Alec will take the guest room at the end of the hall, next to the bathroom"

"Al… ec… live… here?"

"No, not really, he is just moving in for the time being. I had to tell him about our arrangement, so I woke early this morning and knocked on his cabin door. He doesn't like the idea of me staying here, even if it is only temporary. He feels it would be safer for me if he moved in so he can keep an eye on things."

Since Alec was nowhere in sight, I seized the opportunity to question her further about her relationship with him.

"You… love… him?"

"I guess I do, but it's not that romantic kind of love you read about in books. I don't think I'm capable of experiencing that 'soul mate,' 'love you till I die' kind of love."

"Why?"

"I not know. Maybe I'm just too plain. Men don't seem to be attracted to me. You certainly never loved me; and Alec, well, I'm comfortable with Alec. He treats me respectfully and with kindness. I always wanted a family, so when Alec asked me to marry him, I accepted. Once you sign the divorce papers, we are leaving and starting our new life together."

I hoped that day would never come. I wanted her here, with me. I yearned for Ally, but I would settle for Abigail.

"I got up early this morning and wrote down times on the schedule you gave me. I figured we would work on your speech therapy every morning after breakfast. We should be finished by noon. Then, after lunch, we can spend an hour or so going over old photo albums and papers in hopes of getting your memory back. That will leave me some time before dinner to interview secretaries."

"Sec… sec… Why?"

"I can't stay here forever. I need to get back to my own life. I figured a good secretary or gentlemen's gentleman would be the best person to take my place."

I was beginning to see the biggest difference between my Ally and this Abigail. Abigail, though nice, had no intention of keeping me as part of her life. Ally knew she was the reason I existed.

Frustrated, I said, "A…lone… Sh…shower."

"Oh, silly me. This has been a lot to take in. I'll leave you to freshen up before dinner." And she left the room.

I walked to the bathroom at the end of the hall just like I did every morning in 2000. I undressed, turned on the shower, and stepped in, letting the warm water run over me in an effort to wash away the memories haunting me. I stood there until the water ran cold and I felt halfway human again. I tied a towel around my waist and pulled on a striped silk robe before returning to my room.

I opened the door only to be greeted by more ghostly memories still haunting the space. I pictured Ally greeting me at the door as we slowly circled one another in a ritual morning dance. I took a deep breath and walked back to my room. I striped off the silk robe, letting it drape across a corner of the bed, and looked around the room, pulling more memories to the surface. I saw Ally standing in the morning light of my mind, dawn filtering through her black lace nightgown, silhouetting every contour of her body. She stood motionless, innocent, desirable, and delicious. Lost, I didn't here Abigail enter my room through the open door.

"Oh my God!"

I looked over my shoulder to see Abigail's shocked face as she walked toward me.

"Your back, you really were tortured. I thought you might be faking your injuries or at least playing up their severity to win my compassion, but I never expected anything like this."

She stood behind me, lightly tracing each scar with her fingers.

Standing still was easy. I could take the sensation of her fingers outlining the ridges of built-up scare tissue. I had no feeling there. It was when her fingers feathered the soft pink tissue between the scars I was truly tortured. Her touch sent electricity coursing through my veins. The blood pulled from my head and pounded into my heart. I wanted her.

"Stop," I said when I could take no more. I reached for the robe on the bed and quickly put it on, cinching it closed. "What... do... you... want?"

"I forgot to give you a copy of the schedule I wrote out. I have all the days marked on it from now until the end of the year, and you can check them off as we complete them."

"Thank... you."

I took the white folded paper from her hand and escorted her from my room, closing the door. I knew she must have thought my behavior was rude, but I couldn't stand being that close to her without touching her. I knew I needed time to compose myself before I saw her again.

Chapter 27

Beaten

I may have been home, but monotonous was the only word to describe the next few weeks of my existence. Every day I woke, showered, and ate breakfast alone. Abigail and Alec were always careful to share breakfast together before I came downstairs.

After breakfast, I met Abigail in the den for therapy. At first, Alec would hover around us, but as time passed, his confidence in his victory allowed him to leave us alone.

Abigail always remained business-like in my presence. She gave no indication of harboring any feeling for James other than animosity. At first, she insisted the door to the den remain open and there be a desk between us at all times, but eventually she relaxed enough to occasionally touch my arm or tap my shoulder. It was a different story, however, if I attempted to touch her. She recoiled quickly and flashed green fire in her disapproving eyes. I was her pupil and nothing more.

Abigail always took her lunch in her room. She gave no indication of wanting to be social or polite toward James. It was evident she wished to avoid any contact with me as much as possible. There was so much I wanted to tell her, but small, simple, stuttered words were all I was able to produce.

Our after-lunch memory sessions seemed more relaxed. She would take out an old family photo album and lose herself in the stories behind each picture. I couldn't have cared less about what she was saying. I just loved the sound of her voice. It was at these times she most resembled my Ally.

After our memory sessions, she would return to her room or retire to the kitchen to begin preparing the evening supper. Supper was the one meal we all shared together. We ate in the dining room, more formally, as was the custom of the time. Alec and Abigail would converse about the events of the day, and neither one of them made an effort to include me.

After dinner, Alec and I sat in the parlor while Abigail did the dishes. The radio's nightly programs were the only sound echoing through the first floor since neither Alec nor I had any use for one another. Abigail sat in a small armchair, occupying her time knitting or doing needlepoint. At ten PM we turned off the parlor lights and retired to our individual bedrooms for the night. This pattern repeated over and over again like constricting circles, enfolding me, choking me, and squeezing the life out of me.

The repetitive pattern made me numb, but I continued the repetition, looking for some way to break through Abigail and release the Ally I knew lay buried deep within her. I carried a pad of paper and pen into each memory-jogging session. I may not have been able to speak more than a few words, but my writing was more eloquent. Perhaps I could reach her with my words.

I followed her into the den one afternoon to peruse another album for our memory-jogging session. I watched as she stretched to retrieve a large book from the top shelf. I knew it would be nearly impossible for her to pull the book down let alone reach it without hurting herself, so I quickly stretched my arm over her head to get it.

She dropped to the floor, coiled into a ball at my feet, and covered her face with her hands. She was expecting James to hit her. She was used to James hitting her.

I choked back the rage and bile I tasted at the thought of James beating her. I mashed my fist against the bookcase and said, "No more."

I was not my intention to traumatize her further, but my outburst caused Abigail to crawl backward from me in fear. Realizing the terror I caused her, I dropped to my knees to face her more calmly.

"I… am… so… sorry. I… will… never… hit… you. Promise."

She swallowed and took a deep breath. She slowly stood, never taking her suspicious eyes off me.

"I knew I shouldn't trust you. You seemed fine when you first got here, but somehow I knew you would eventually return to your old ways. I was fine with you not remembering anything about being James. I almost began to trust you again. But now, each day you get closer to being the James I knew, the James that married me to get my father's business, the James that always took his anger out on me, the James that destroyed the only thing good to come out of this marriage, the James that just hit the bookcase. I won't let you hurt me again. Please, just let me go."

"No… please." I reached for my paper and wrote.

I am so sorry. I only wanted to help you get the book down. I was just as shocked by your reaction as you were by my move. I didn't mean to startle you. Please forgive me.

"Alright, you can get the book down. We will go over it today, but you have to remain on one side of the desk and the door will stay open or I'll scream for Alec."

I crossed my heart and raised my palm, swearing to be on my best behavior. I took down the album, handed it to her, and took my place as she directed.

"Before we begin, I want you to know, I plan on engaging a secretary for you and leaving before the week is out. I refuse to be anywhere near you when the real James returns for good."

She opened the album containing pictures of James and Abigail's wedding and life together.

I wrote my first question down and slid the pad of paper to her.

Tell me about our marriage.

"There isn't much to tell. You married me to get my father's business. I was just a pawn to get you what you wanted. You didn't care for me one way or the other."

Was there ever any love between us?

"I don't think so."

The picture of James and Abigail's wedding made it quite clear that James was too taken with himself to ever care about someone else. It was strange to see the physical similarities between James and myself. Genetics could explain how Abigail looked so much like Ally; after all, they were related. But why did I look like James? Maybe the pictures weren't very focused and left too much to the imagination, or maybe Abigail and Ally were attracted to the same type of man.

She turned the pages to reveal James and Abigail's honeymoon. They had gone to Niagara Falls, as was the custom in those days. I found it strange; there were many pictures of the falls, but none of James and Abigail together.

How was our honeymoon?

"I guess you could say it was different."

I wanted to ask about Abigail and James' lovemaking, but the propriety of the day only allowed me to write:

Didn't we spend a good deal of our time in our room?

Her answer surprised me. "Do you want to know what it was like making love with you?"

I nodded, but her demeanor grew cold rather than nostalgic.

"I was a virgin when we married. You, on the other hand, had plenty of experience. I hoped you would be kind, caring, patient, and instruct when we were together. What you were was drunk. So, on our wedding night, you more or less had your way and then left me in our room. I knew you had no interest in me because shortly after we returned from our honeymoon, you began to find reasons to stay away. I finally realized you never wanted me. You had other women."

You said I destroyed the best part of our marriage. What was it?

"The baby… You didn't sleep with me often, but you did get me pregnant. I would have been happy to raise the child on my own, but you were too selfish even for that."

What happened?

"You were furious when you found out about the baby. You exploded and dragged me up to the top of the stairs. I tried to plead with you and calm you down, but you hit me and I fell backward down the flight of stairs. I lost the baby, to your relief, and I vowed that day I would leave you. I was still recovering from my miscarriage when you decided to go off to war and play the hero. I waited and hoped for a quick divorce as soon as you returned, but then we received word you were missing in action. You know what happened after that."

I could feel her pain. James had caused her to miscarry just like I had caused Ally to lose our baby. I didn't blame her for wanting to leave James, but I needed her to stay.

Do you still want to leave me?

"I've held up my end of the bargain. Yes, I want to leave. Please sign the divorce papers, and Alec and I will be out of here by morning."

Please, just a few more days.

"I'll give you until the end of the week."

With that she stood and walked out of the room, leaving behind a cold emptiness.

Chapter 28

Skylight

The end of the week and the end of any chance I had to win Abby over hung over me with impending doom. I had to do something, anything, to keep Abigail from leaving, but what? I had tried being gentle and caring, but she always pulled away. I had tried to draw her to me with words, but her stone heart couldn't hear me. I had tried to jog her memory within the magical places around the manor, but only I could see the ghostly pieces of our life together.

I had tried everything I could think of, except one thing. I had not kissed her yet. Maybe if I could get her to relax long enough to let me get that close, it could be the key to my salvation. But why would she ever trust James enough to let him be intimate?

I lay in bed, sleepless, pondering Tom's theory. If Ally did remember who she was and stayed with me, I would erase everything about her in the future.

Abigail was supposed to divorce James and marry Alec. Their child would be Ally's grandmother. Without that genetic connection, Ally would not exist. I could win her back only to ultimately lose her. My mind rocked between my choices: have Abby stay with me and lose Ally in the future or let Abby go to be with Alec. Need finally won out over common sense. I had to get Ally to remember me, no matter the cost.

I sat up in my bed and turned on the lamp. I had read just about very volume contained in the meager library downstairs, and the last novel on my nightstand did not intrigue me, so I decided to roam around the manor.

I opened the door of my room and stepped into the hall. I could see a light bleeding out from the crack of Abigail's bedroom door. I wondered if she even realized I was the piece missing, the piece that caused her mind to deprive her body of nightly slumber.

I stole silently down the staircase and into the kitchen to get a glass of milk.

Abigail sat at the table, staring out the darkened window into the night. A small flickering candle was her only companion.

The lighting was identical to the lighting that night, the last time I had Ally in my arms. I could still see Ally's tear-streaked face and her pleading aqua-green eyes as I kissed her salty lips and pushed her into Tom's waiting grip. Abigail now sat only inches from that same spot. Having Ally so close yet so far away tore me apart.

She turned to look at me with weary eyes. "You can't sleep either?" She didn't wait for me to reply. "I used to sleep just fine until your mother passed away. She was such a nice lady. She made me promise to look for you. I could never understand why. You didn't treat her any better than you treated me. But I loved her, so I did. It was a few days after that when I began having trouble sleeping. Now it seems to be every night.

You know, it's funny, the only time I remember getting a good night's sleep was at the train station and on the boat with you. I don't know why that would be. We barely tolerate each other."

I poured some milk in a glass and sat down opposite her, not speaking. I wondered if she realized that it was my Ally inside of her causing her not to sleep. I knew my reason for insomnia was that I would never be completely at peace unless Ally was at my side.

"Milk?" I stammered.

"No, thank you. I must have drank a gallon of warm milk. Nothing helps. I can't stand just laying in my bed waiting for morning, so I come down here or roam the halls. Would you like to see my favorite place to be at night? It is silly, but it's the only place in this whole house I feel comfortable."

"Yes."

She stood and signaled me to follow her up the back stairs of the house to the third floor. I walked a step behind as she led the way to the space that someday would be our home. I prayed that opening the door would open a floodgate of memories for her.

She opened the door, revealing an unfinished attic filled with musty old trunks and dusty boxes. It looked nothing like the home we shared in the future. She led us through the long maze of discarded possessions and walked directly to the place that someday would be our bathroom.

The attic space was chilled by the clear, cold, late fall night. Moonlight shining down from the original skylight washed the floor in light. I could see on an old mattress covered in layers of blankets, quilts, and several pillows on the floor under the skylight.

A faint trail of steam blew from her lips when she spoke. "I like to come here and look at the stars and the moon moving overhead. I guess I rationalize being at peace is almost as good as sleeping." She laughed and sat down on the mattress. "Do you know anything about the stars?"

I sat down on the mattress beside her and looked up through the skylight. I located the only band of stars I knew for certain. Pointing, I said "O…rion."

She laid down, nestling her form into the cotton bedding. "I only know the North Star, over there. I think it's called Polaris," she said, pointing.

I cautiously stretch my body out next to hers. Lying still and so close to her was unnerving. I wanted, needed to smell the scent of her skin, to feel her body close to mine, to experience her, but I had to be careful how I approached her.

I turned my head to look at her bathed in her own personal light. The moonlight made her lips an inviting shade of plum. Her hair fanned out into a golden halo around her. Her arms rested above her head like a ballet dancer in pirouette.

I raised myself up on one elbow and leaned toward her.

My movement caught her attention, and she turned her head to look at me. There was a passion in her eyes I had not seen before.

I leaned over her and caught her wrists in my hand, letting the weight of my body press against her. I made a trail of soft kisses from her ear to her neck with my lips. I breathed in the taste of her, leaning into a kiss. And then I felt the shiver of panic rush through her.

She began to scream and hit at me violently.

"Let go of my hands. Get off of me. Let me go or I'll scream for Alec."

I would have let her go, but this violent outburst took me by surprise. I was too stunned to move.

She began to kick and squirm her way out from under me. I rolled onto my back to free her, and she jumped to her feet and stared down at me.

I took her hand and gently pulled to bring her back to my side, but she jerked it away and ran from the attic screaming Alec's name.

I followed her, hoping to calm her down. Why would such a tender moment frighten her so terribly? Was James guilty of more than hitting her? Could he have raped her also?

She raced down the stairs to the kitchen, continually screaming Alec's name.

I ran behind her, hoping to catch her and explain I would never hurt her like that, but all I could do was watch as she jumped into Alec's waiting arms. I felt the force of his blow slam into me, and I crashed backward into the stairs.

I looked up to see Alec—or Tom—forming an impenetrable wall between Abigail and I.

He turned his back to me and spoke to Abigail. "You are okay now. I won't let him hurt you. Go back to your room. I'll take care of him." He kissed her on her forehead, and she obeyed his request as if hypnotized by the sound of his voice.

Once she left the kitchen, he turned his sights on me. "You really are making my job so much easier than I ever hoped."

"Job?" I asked.

"Don't you pay attention? You and she can never be. It's my job to make sure it never happens. That is why I was sent here. The powers of the twenty-third century sent me to retrieve you, but what if I could get rid of Ally as well? I really would be a hero then. My orders were to stop the two of you from procreating any way I could. At first, I thought of finding you and just killing you. But what if you left her pregnant? I then planned to kill her, but she is very sweet, almost endearing, don't you think? And then it dawned on me. I could seduce her to follow me anywhere I wanted. Taking her from a boy like you would be easy. She didn't have to have your child. She could have mine. It was easy enough to get her away from you. She trusted me. And then the leap into this time, well, it couldn't have been a more perfect set-up. You see, James, you have beaten and raped and abused poor Abigail to a point where she will never trust you. After what ever you did to her tonight, I'm sure she'll agree to leave with me tomorrow. So it's good-bye, James. Or should I say, David?" With that, he turned and walked out of the kitchen, laughing.

I wasn't going to let what he said stop me. Maybe Abigail hated and feared James, but Ally was in her somewhere, and Ally loved me. Of that I was certain.

Chapter 29

Parting

I spent the rest of the night thinking of ways I could win back the little trust Abigail had for me. My mind raced in circles, driving me insane. I knew Ally was in Abigail. She just had to be. Why would God bring us so close together only to tear us apart? I was desperate. I had to do something to stop her from leaving, but what?

When the first shimmer of dawn trickled into my room, I left to search for Abigail and apologize, but she was nowhere to be found. I moved from room to room in the emptiness of the manor, but no signs of Abigail or Alec were to be found. I could taste the panic within me. Was I too late? Had she left as she said she would? Was I really left to live without her?

I heard the front door open and looked down the staircase to the first floor.

Alec walked in first, with Abigail close behind. He took off his coat and then helped Abigail off with hers. He hung them in the entryway closet and then took Abby's hand and walked into the kitchen.

I quickly descended the staircase to join them.

"I... am... sorry... about... last night," I said upon entering. It was an effort to say just these few words, but writing them down instead didn't seem prudent.

Alec shot a cold, steely glare at me. "I have already found a place for Abigail and I. I took her this morning to show her the place. I take full blame for what happened last night. I should have known better than to leave her alone with you."

Abby, however, looked at me with tender green-blue eyes and said, "It's all right. I told you before we didn't have that kind of a marriage. I guess I was just fooling myself thinking you wouldn't return to your old ways so soon. It was my fault things got out of hand."

"Leaving?" I wanted to say so much more to her, but the distortion in my speech and the barrier of Alec between us prevented me.

Abby spoke. "Yes, we will be leaving this evening. I have an interview for a butler at six. I feel it is my responsibility to stay and explain all your personal needs to him, but after that we will be going."

"Work… today… with… me." I hoped Abigail and I could have some time to talk to each other alone before she disappeared completely.

"I've left the two of you alone much too much. I will not let her out of my sight anymore, so therapy is off for today," Alec said, scooping his arm around her and pulling her from the room.

Alec stayed true to his word. He shadowed every move Abigail made. I wondered if he might fear she was remembering Ally, but as the hours ticked by, I realized it was more to torture me. Alec had a sick, vindictive nature, and watching the only reason I had to live drain from me like sand pouring in an hourglass gave him satisfaction.

At six o'clock, the doorbell of the manor rang. Abigail floated down the staircase and opened the door to a short, balding, middle-aged man. She escorted him into the den with Alec still shadowing behind and closed the door.

I remained in my room, powerless to the events unfolding around me.

Alec stood in my doorway announcing, "You can come downstairs now. Abigail wants to introduce you to your new housemate. It does my heart good to know I won't be leaving you all alone, little brother. You'll have this great big house and a butler to serve your every need, and I'll have Abigail to serve my every need. Sometimes life can be beautiful."

I pushed past his smug exterior and made my way down to the den. I walked in, and the middle-aged man stood, extending his hand to me.

Abigail began making the introductions. "This is Lewis."

I grabbed a paper and pen from the desk and wrote.

Is Lewis his first name or last?

"It really doesn't matter does it? You don't care about people, so I'm sure you will just call him Lewis. I have given him all the instructions necessary, and he will be moving in tomorrow morning. I told him he could have the room Alec has now. I have also instructed him to move your things into your mother's old room. It's only fair you have the master bedroom when I leave."

She turned to Lewis. "I will leave you and Alec to go over the contract for your employment. He will also give you a key to the house and show you your room. It has been a pleasure to meet you, sir." She shook hands with Lewis and went upstairs to pack.

Alec and Lewis sat down and started to conduct their business, and I stole the opportunity to follow Abby. I stopped in my room, found the divorce papers, and signed James Stevens on the bottom. Then I headed for her room. Maybe if I came with a peace offering she would be more receptive to listening.

I stood in the doorway and waited for her to realize I was there. I knew surprising her from behind would do me no good.

"What do you want?"

"I… have… a… gift.. for… you."

"A gift," she said suspiciously. "What kind of a gift? Is it another trick? What are you thinking in that devious mind of yours?"

"No," I said softly. I held out the papers to her.

It wasn't until she took the papers from my hand that the inevitability of my fate tore into me. She was leaving forever, and I knew her absence would destroy me. I would be unable to live without her soul proving my existence. I wanted to die.

"I don't believe it. You actually signed them. I'm free? I can go?"

I nodded yes, but I could feel the hope of ever getting Ally back being sucked out of me like blood pouring out an open wound. What was I to do when she left? I couldn't stay here in 1940. Any time without her would be no time to live. With tears welling in my eyes, I took one last move toward her. This would be the last time I would ever be alone with Ally, and I had to say good-bye.

I slowly reached out my hand. She didn't pull away, so I stepped closer. I could hear Romeo's last words somewhere in the back of my mind.

Eyes, look you last! Arms, take your last embrace! And lips, O the doors of breath, seal this dateless bargain to engrossing death.

I knew at that moment I could not live, I would not live, without her. I would not have to commit suicide. I was certain the pain of living without the heart she took with her would swiftly ensure my demise.

I stared down into her aquamarine eyes, and she stood motionless, staring back. I brushed my hand along her cheek and caught up her hair, closing my fingers around it. I gently tugged down on her hair, raising her face to mine for the last time, and then I let my lips press down on hers. I drank in as much of her as I could, knowing this was the end. My heart flashed blood and electricity through every fiber of my being, but she stood stone cold like a statue. I was kissing Ally good-bye, but Abigail couldn't care less. I stopped my kiss and loosened my hold on her hair, stepping back for one last look.

She stood motionless, just staring blankly. I feared I must have snapped something in her. She looked catatonic, not even breathing.

"Abigail?" I whispered.

She took in a deep breath, keeping her eyes locked on mine. Tears welled in her eyes, rolling down over the contours of her face, but she still did not move.

She raised her trembling arm slowly until it rested against my cheek.

"David?" she sobbed out.

Now it was my turn to stop breathing. The blood rushed from my head, surging wildly into my chest.

"Oh my God, David?" Her fingers traced my face in a sensual inventory.

I pulled her close to me, kissed the tips of her fingers, and moved to kiss her again, but this time I was kissing Allyson. I could feel her. I said her name, "Ally," licking her lips.

I wanted to hold her tightly against me forever, but she walked slowly past me to the door. I let my fingers trace down her shoulder, then her arm, and finally to the tips of her fingers, not wishing to let her even an inch from me.

She shut the bedroom and turned the key, locking us in. She turned to look at me.

"Oh my God, David, I missed you."

I opened my arms, and she rushed back into them. We kissed passionately, Ally and David, no longer James and Abigail.

"I want you so badly," I said.

"I want you too," she replied enticingly.

"You know we aren't really married. Do you have a problem with that?"

"James and Abby are married."

"We are not James and Abby."

"We are for now."

"I can't, not here, not with Alec a few feet away."

"David, your voice, you're not stuttering!"

"I'm not. I guess it just more proof I can't exist completely without you."

She unbuttoned my shirt, tracing her fingers on my chest and driving me to heavenly distraction. She picked up the crystal around my neck and studied it, reflective in her hand.

"This crazy, terrible crystal, it brought us together, but it also helped in tearing us apart."

I took the crystal from around my neck and threw it onto the bed. "I don't need to be in any time but here with you." I kissed her again, but this time more deeply. "There is only one place I want to take you to make love to you."

"The attic?" she winked.

Chapter 30

ONYX

Things were different when I opened my eyes.

"Things were different" was an understatement.

The skylight above my head still canopied the sky, but it was the soft blue sky of a spring day. I remembered falling asleep the night before to light snow wisped across it.

The most significant difference was the beauty I lay next to. If I touched her, she turned to me, even in her sleep. If I positioned by body further from her, she quickly filled the gap and nestled against me. And if I touched her lips, her mouth opened in response. This was Ally with all traces of Abigail gone. I propped myself up on one elbow and covered Ally's eyes with my other hand, partly to shield her from the shower of morning light streaming down on her from the open sunlight, and partly to prepare her for what she was about to witness.

"Ally."

She bent toward the sound of my voice, still asleep.

"Ally," I whispered in her ear.

"Mmm," she moaned, cuddling closer to me. "Why is your hand over my eyes? Are we playing 'guess who I am'? I know who you are. You're my David."

"I'm glad you remember. No, I just wanted to prepare you before you opened your eyes."

"Prepare me for what?"

"Things are a little different."

"How different? You're scaring me."

"Just different." I lifted my hand from her eyes, slowly.

At first she blinked against the strong morning light. Then she sat up looking around in disbelief. She took in the panorama of our surroundings: It was our home, our attic apartment. The only traces of 1940 were the blankets we had fallen asleep cocooned in. We had entered the night under a skylight in 1940, laying on a hardwood floor, and awoke in our porcelain Jacuzzi tub seventy years in the future.

She turned her eyes back to me and said in amazement, "We're home? How? Did you leap us after I fell asleep?"

"No, my crystal is still downstairs where I left it."

"Then how?"

"I have no idea, but there's more."

"More? I'm afraid to ask."

"Well, for one thing, where is Alec— I mean Tom? I locked the door to the attic behind us last night, but that wouldn't have stopped him from finding us. Where is he?"

"I don't care where he is. He can't tear us apart anymore. I won't let him."

I smiled. "There's something else."

"What?"

I sat up wrapped in a blanket and stepped out of the tub. I sat on the edge of the chilled porcelain with my back toward her and let the blanket fall.

She gasped. "Your back, your beautiful back, there are no more scars."

"I guess they belonged to James."

She ran her fingers tracing the contours of my back and softly pressed her warm moist lips against my spine, making a trail of sensual kisses.

"You better stop that or it will take at least another hour to get out of this bathroom," I begged.

"Sorry, I just can't seem to get enough of you."

"Believe me, the feeling is mutual." I stood up and held out my hand to her. She gracefully stepped out of our tub and onto the marbled bathroom floor. She followed me as I opened the door to our bedroom.

We stepped in, still amazed by the fact that we feel asleep in each other arms in an unfinished attic in 1940 and awoke in our attic apartment in 2010.

"Let's get dressed and see if the rest of the house is back as well," I suggested.

"Putting clothes on you would be like covering Michelangelo's David. By the way, is that how you got your name?"

"Very funny. I like what you're *not* wearing also, but we have to get dressed if we are ever to open the attic door."

"All right, you win."

We each threw on the first T-shirt and jeans we could find and continued our trek through the apartment. The great room was still the same as the first night I showed it to her. Not even a throw pillow was out of place. The only added feature was the smell of coffee and pancakes beckoning us from just outside the door.

Ally took in a deep breath of the delicious aroma. "Samantha! Samantha must be here. I know I didn't remember her when I was Abigail, but a piece of me missed her. Do you think she and Don are back as well?"

"There is only one way to find out."

We walked to our apartment door, looked at each other, and took a deep breath opening it. We grabbed each other's hand and headed down the stairs to the kitchen.

Don was seated at the kitchen island reading the morning paper and drinking his coffee. Sam sat across from him, facing us.

She stood up when we walked in and asked, "Can I get you something to eat?"

I could feel the shock run through Ally at the sight of Samantha.

Ally stepped toward Sam, holding out her hand in disbelief, resting it on Samantha's swollen pregnant belly.

"How could…" She stopped herself and quickly covered, "How do you feel?"

"I feel great, but this one," touching her stomach, "is a little active today."

Ally turned to me, and we looked at each other, confused.

"We could use some coffee," I said, forcing myself to reply to Sam's initial question as effortlessly as possible.

I sat down next to Don and signaled for Ally to join me. I craned my neck to see the date on the newspaper blocking my brother. It said April 13, 2009. It was just three days after our wedding.

"Are you planning on going to work today with me, or are you two still on your honeymoon?" Don said jokingly.

"Work?" I asked.

"Yes, work, little brother. That is how we pay for all of this."

"Refresh my memory. Where do we work?"

"What are you drunk with love? We work at the university. You teach history, and I teach science. Look, if you plan on playing hooky again today, you'll have to call for a sub yourself. I covered for you the last three days, but no more."

"I'll call." I was still amazed by what was happening. It seemed surreal. It was obvious I couldn't go to work today. I couldn't leave Ally in the midst of the mystery surrounding us.

"You left this in our room." Samantha reached into the pocket of her robe and took out my crystal, dropping it in my open palm.

"You know about this?" I questioned.

"I know you and Don keep them locked up. So be more careful. It was on the floor in our room, and I almost stepped on it this morning."

I looked at Ally, returning her puzzled glance. Don had always insisted on keeping the secret of our crystals from Sam, and now she was casually discussing them.

Ally stood up and went back to Sam's side. She helped her pour two cups of coffee and stacked a few pancakes onto two plates. Ally turned and placed the coffee and plates on the island and sat back down next to me.

The four of us talked about inane things like the news and weather. It felt comfortable to be back together, almost like we had never been apart.

I hated to see this come to an end, but I needed to find the answers to the questions racing through my head. I motioned to Ally with my eyes, and we returned to our apartment.

As soon as we were alone, Ally said, "I don't understand what is happening."

"I don't know either. I think we might have changed history, but I can't be sure until I check on something."

I sat down at the desk in the great room and turned on the computer. Ally sat in my lap while I waited for it to load up. I filtered through the papers thrown on the desktop, finding the normal household bills, but one paper buried on the bottom looked different. I pulled it out and read it, then looked at Ally and said, "It's my traveling papers. My leap was approved by the government of the twenty-third century. I didn't spore. I'm here with permission. That would explain why Tom isn't here. If I'm legally able to time travel, there would be no need to send a falcon out to find me." I showed the document to Ally.

"So, what, it's okay for you to be here now? No one— I mean, no falcons— are coming to get us?"

"That's what I think. I'm not a spore, and you aren't a Halo."

"Then I'm not special anymore?"

"You will always be special to me. But it appears the twenty-third century doesn't need us to breed people. I guess babies in the future are still made the old-fashioned way. It explains how Samantha is pregnant."

The laptop was ready, so I logged on to geneology.com.

"What are you looking for?"

"I'm looking for your family tree."

"Why?"

"I think I know now what happened."

"What? What happened?"

"We changed history."

"How?"

"I think I left Abigail pregnant... See?" I said pointing to the screen.

She peered down to view her family tree. She perused each entry carefully. "I still don't know what I'm looking for."

"It's right here," I said, pointing to the screen.

"What's right there? Abigail Bentley was married to James Stevens and had a daughter, Melissa? I still don't see it."

Melissa is your grandmother. And her last name was Stevens."

"So?"

"Until last night, Melissa's last name was Denby, not Stevens. Alec or Tom told me he was sent to get you. He could have just taken you against your will, but he decided seducing you into going with him would be easier. He set up the whole urgency for us to leap and picked our time destination. He knew that leaping with you would erase your memory, making it easier for him to be Melissa's father. But when you returned to me last night, I guess your choice changed history. I'm your great grandfather, in theory."

"That's not funny."

"I think us making love last night *did* leave James and Abigail together and Abigail pregnant. It would explain why there is no Alec or Tom in the picture anymore. Tom would not be looking for you. Your DNA has changed. James Stevens is your great grandfather now, not Alec Denby."

"So we are safe? No one will come looking for us?"

"It appears so."

She wrapped her arms around my neck and pulled me into a kiss.

I could taste the relief on her lips. We were safe and together for all time. There was one thing left I had to do. I stood up with her in my arms and twisted to place her back in the desk chair.

"Wait right here. I have something for you." I went to the kitchen and reached for a small, white plastic bag hidden on the top shelf of one of the cabinets. Once I had it in my hands, I returned to her.

"I bought this just before we got married. I hid it thinking it would be a great Christmas gift for you, but I think you should have it now." I took out the black velvet jewel box and handed it to her.

She opened it and lifted a black onyx pendant out. The silver back reflected circles of colored light as the pendant spun from the chain she held laced in her fingers. She stopped the movement to read the engraving on the back. "Onyx?"

"Read the card."

She took out the small white card pushed into the top of the black box, unfolded it, and read:

I Only Need You to eXist

I took the pendant from her hand, opened the clasp, and hung it from her neck.

She clasped it in her hand and said, "It is beautifully perfect, just like you. I'll never take it off."

I then placed my hand on her stomach and looked down at her. "How do you feel about being a mother?"

"It's okay. Why?"

"Well, what if Abigail wasn't the only one I left pregnant last night?"

"Let's not take any chances." She smiled, stood, and raced to the bedroom, pulling me after her.